"All I'm asking you to do is not discount anything. Stick around for a while longer and try out the product," Matt said.

"The product?" Kate frowned. "You mean the island?"

"I mean me. I'm the product."

"Do you come with a guarantee?"

Matt laughed. "If not completely satisfied, return for a full refund."

"I just might take you up on that."

He lifted his wineglass into the air. "To whatever comes."

Kate clinked her glass against his. "Whatever."

"Don't be so blasé," he said coolly. "I just might sweep you off your feet. Besides," he added, "I'm not blind, you know."

"Blind to what?"

"That dress. Your hair. Everything." His eyes swept over her, clearly indicating that he liked what he saw.

"Let your defenses down, Kate," he said softly. "I won't bite . . ."

Diana Morgan

Diana Morgan is a pseudonym for a husband-and-wife team who only moonlight as writers. By day they are two of New York's busiest literary agents. They met at a phone booth at Columbia University in 1977, and have been together romantically and professionally ever since.

"We began writing together strictly by accident," they confess, "deriving our pen name from our cat, Dinah Cat Morgenstern." Writing turned out to be a welcome form of comic relief from the pressures of business.

"This is a wonderful opportunity for us to talk directly to you, the reader. Our books have often been described as humorous or zany, but we feel there is an underlying seriousness to even our craziest story. What we hope to convey is a certain joie de vivre that will escape from the pages into a part of your life."

The "Morgans" enjoy all kinds of music, pigging out, small children and elves (especially their children, Robbie and Elizabeth), and trying to figure out what will happen next on Dallas.

SECOND CHANCE AT LOVE™

DIANA MORGAN
WORLDS APART

B
BERKLEY BOOKS, NEW YORK

First edition published December 1989

ISBN: 0-425-11885-1

"Second Chance at Love" and the butterfly emblem are trademarks belonging to Jove Publications, Inc. The name "BERKLEY" and the "B" logo are trademarks belonging to Berkley Publishing Corporation.

Second Chance at Love books are published by
The Berkley Publishing Group
200 Madison Avenue, New York, NY 10016

Printed in the United States of America

10 9 8 7 6 5 4 3 2 1

WORLDS APART

CHAPTER
One

BLACKWELL'S ISLAND, twenty miles off the coast of Maine, has a double personality. It has a summer resort population of fifty thousand, but when the season is over it drops to a winter low of less than three thousand. December means it's time to hibernate. In summer or winter, though, the best place to be was Kate's Tavern.

Thirty-one-year-old Kate Brody, the proprietor of the tavern, was something of a mystery, even though she had been a year-round resident for three years. She simply showed up one day in the middle of January, piloting her own boat across the twenty miles of frigid ocean. Old Flint, the tavern's former owner, was the first to see her making her way into the harbor that freezing morning. No one knows why, but he offered her a job. It was enough that she had appeared. Anyone crazy or desperate enough to come to Blackwell's Island in the dead of winter was welcome to stay, no questions asked. The trip alone was proof of intent.

Flint let her have the room behind the bar. When he retired a year later, Kate bought the tavern from him, thereby confirming her status as an island regular. By that time a few rumors had circulated about her past—something about a disastrous love affair and a job that had abruptly terminated—but again, no one asked any direct questions. It was part of the unspoken code of the island: anyone foolish enough to live there all year was entitled to his idiosyncracies and his privacy.

The tavern, of course, remained what it had always been—the only gathering place and meeting hall on the island for over three hundred years. Anything that has happened or can or will happen on Blackwell's Island starts right there at Kate's.

But the truth is that hardly anything ever does happen, especially in January. Hardly anyone or anything comes onto the island. The ferry stops running because of the ice in the harbor, the planes can't land because of snow and high winds, and anyone without a snowmobile or a cat tractor disappears until the first thaw in March.

Digger's General Store stocks extra canned goods, and once a week a helicopter from the coast brings fresh supplies and mail. The only other businesses that stay open are Jack's Auto Repair, the liquor store, the dry cleaners, the pharmacy, and the VCR rental store.

This January would have been no different than any other if three remarkable events hadn't occurred. And they all happened in the same evening.

The first was that Kate Brody put a FOR SALE sign in the window of the tavern just as the last light left the sky. The second was that not ten minutes later, Sheriff

Caine received a five-day-old telegram from his daughter that sent him straight to a stool in Kate's bar for the first time in his life. And the third was that George Digger saw a flying saucer crash into Stan Farquil's brand-new barn.

Kate had been hiding in her office after putting up the FOR SALE sign. She knew it would cause something of a furor, since she hadn't told anyone of her intent. There were no customers in the bar, but there would be any moment. Sundown was the unofficial end of the workday on the island, the time when everyone began to saunter in.

The door slammed and, much to her surprise, Sheriff Matthew Caine stomped inside, shaking the snow from his down parka. He was the last person she ever expected to see in her place. Their long-standing feud over everything from parking permits to brawls and noise levels had been the sum of their relationship, what there was of it. Kate had insisted that the noise level in a tavern should be unlimited, and that an occasional brawl was good for business. Matt had routinely squelched all such diversions, once actually issuing her a summons when she refused to comply. Kate had allowed people to park their cars right up on the sidewalk in front of the tavern, knowing there was no place else to put them when it got crowded. Matt had slapped her with a fine each time.

She couldn't understand why he remained such a popular figure in town when he was so by-the-book conservative. Of course, he was reliable. Even she couldn't deny that. He was always there when someone had a medical emergency, or when a car got stuck in the snow late at night, or when anyone needed to get a message off the island and the phones were down. His passion for rules and regulations was just one of those idiosyncracies that everyone accepted, she guessed. Well, it was no longer any of her concern. She was leaving.

Reluctantly she came out of her tiny office and went behind the bar as Matt threw his parka onto the coatrack and plunked down on the nearest stool. A customer was a customer.

"What'll it be?" she asked without looking at him.

"Bourbon. Straight up."

Now she did look up. This was practically historic. Not only had Matt Caine never socially frequented her tavern, when he was there "on business" he never ordered anything stronger than ginger ale. "You sure?"

He nodded, catching her eye to make sure she knew he meant it. There was determination in his face, but there was also something else. She paused for a second to examine it. His face was ruddy and strong, marked with clear lines that represented a wealth of experience. His eyes were vividly blue—too blue for such an impossibly stubborn man, she thought—and they had a tendency to twinkle with suppressed amusement as if at some inside joke. This quality had always unnerved her, and it unnerved her now.

"What is it, Matt?" she asked directly. "I can tell you've got something else on your mind."

"You selling this place?" he asked.

So that was it. Of course. The FOR SALE sign was bound to cause a flurry of reaction. "Yes," she answered, enjoying her new role as the bearer of the hottest news in town.

He frowned slightly. "Why?" He had the habit of being very direct, with no frills and no preliminaries. It made her want to look elsewhere, but she couldn't tear her eyes away from the brilliant gaze from those lake-blue eyes.

She shrugged and reached for the bourbon. "It's personal."

He nodded slightly, watching as she poured him a shot. "So you're leaving, just like that?"

She fought the sudden little tremor that went through her as he looked at her. Right to the point, no mincing words. She had always thought that he was devoid of humor, all business with no time for standard small-town chatter. But now she sensed something else in his blunt questions, something that resembled real interest, real concern.

"I'll be leaving as soon as I get a buyer," she said with feigned casualness. "Someone ought to snatch this place up before the season opens. They'll have plenty of time to take possession and take full advantage of the summer profits." She looked down suddenly, unable to face him. There was something so intense about him, something that cut through any layer of defense right to the core.

But he said nothing more, addressing his attention to the shot of bourbon in front of him. He picked it up, held it against the light as if admiring it, then tossed it straight down his throat just as the door banged open and a group of townspeople marched in.

The winter wind blasted through the room for a moment before the door was firmly shut. There was the usual rustle of coats and stamping of boots before the group settled down at the bar.

The first one to notice Matt was Jack Gardner, the town mechanic. "Well, well, will you look at that!" he exclaimed. "It's the sheriff himself, hoisting one like a champ!"

As all eyes turned in Matt's direction, the door opened again, sending the wind sweeping around the place. There in the doorway also staring at Matt in disbelief was Old Flint. "I can't believe my eyes."

Matt grunted. "Shut the damn door, you old fool, before this liquor starts freezing in my veins."

The old man squinted in Matt's direction, marched over to the bar, sat down on the stool next to Matt's, and gave him a hearty slap on the back. "It's about time," he said.

Kate noticed with considerable satisfaction that Matt actually looked embarrassed. "I was toasting the bartender," he informed the group. "In case you didn't notice the sign out front, she's selling the tavern."

Kate winced as the predictable reaction set in. There was a stunned silence, followed by exchanged glances of amazement, followed by the usual Blackwell reticence. "Is that so," Jack offered finally. "Well, congratulations, I guess."

"Thanks." Kate bit back the sudden stab of sadness that assailed her. She would miss Jack. She would miss all of them.

The door banged open again and more people trouped in. The news was spread promptly, Kate was kept busy serving drinks, and Matt actually ordered another shot. She put the entire bottle on the bar and waited with a flourish, letting everyone see that history was being made.

Flint chuckled and hooted as she presented it and everyone laughed. Kate looked closely at Matt. He wasn't smiling.

She leaned with her elbows on the bar. "Lighten up, old man," she tried, teasing him gently.

He sat up straight on the stool and eyed her angrily.

"What do you mean, 'old man'?" he shot back. "I'm only forty-one."

Kate shrugged helplessly. "I— Nothing," she said, cowed. "Don't be so sensitive. I thought you came in to celebrate my departure. You'll finally be rid of wild tavern brawls and parking violations. Blackwell will be blessedly crime-free once again."

He looked at her stonily and picked up the bottle of bourbon. Without missing a beat, he filled his shot glass right to the top, gulped it down, and quickly refilled it.

She stared at him. "It's your funeral, Sheriff. Are you sure . . . ?"

One look from him was enough to silence her. She didn't know how he did it, but he carried a built-in authority that made him seem like much more than the sheriff of Blackwell County. He wasn't more than six-feet tall, and his body was lean and powerful more than it was imposing. But his presence was always heightened by an invisible electricity that told everyone he was in command. Kate always had the uneasy feeling that he had a hidden battalion of troops just waiting to be called into action by their fearless leader.

The bar quieted down and everyone watched except Dan Shere, who was busy depositing a quarter in the jukebox. It clinked loudly and the mechanism whirred as his selection was readied.

Matt slowly brought the glass to his lips, balancing it to keep its contents from spilling over. Kate was fairly sure he was deliberately heightening the sense of drama for his audience, but the effect was abruptly spoiled by a strange sound from outside. It was a cross between a jet plane, a seagull, and a car in need of a new muffler.

Kate looked at Matt, then they both looked up along with everyone else and followed the sound as it moved east to west. It seemed to scream deafeningly as it passed over their heads heading toward the other side of the island.

When it finally passed out of earshot, they all looked at each other.

"What was *that*?"

Suddenly, the door was thrown open and George Digger of Digger's General Store practically fell into the tavern, his eyes wild with shock.

Everyone turned to look at him as he fought to catch his breath. "What is it, George?" Matt asked with his usual practicality. "You look like you've seen a ghost."

"Not . . . a ghost," George said, panting, still out of breath. "A . . . a UFO!"

No one said anything. They all just looked at him quizzically, deciding what to make of this strange announcement, Willie Nelson's "On the Road Again" playing loudly in the background.

"I saw it!" George insisted. "I saw it with my own eyes!"

Jack Gardner nodded a little but still no one said anything. The sheriff winced at the loud music and studied the bourbon glass in his hand without putting it down. "You saw a what?" he asked wearily.

Hal Freedy, pharmacist and self-appointed resident expert, leaned over and supplied, "He said he saw a UFO. That's an unidentified flying object."

George was frantically rubbing his hands together to warm them. "What's the matter with you people? Aren't you listening to me? The darn thing must have been doing Warp Factor Three."

"Warp Factor *what*?" the sheriff asked, raising his voice above the music.

"That's Star Trek lingo," Hal explained. "It means

that it was going faster than the speed of light."

Willie Nelson continued to sing, and Kate began to laugh. "Aw, come on now, George. Lighten up a little. You probably saw a shooting star or an air force jet."

"I have eyes, Miss Kate, and I know what I saw. That was no shooting star or jet. It was long and it had fins and it was shooting a hundred-foot flame from its back end. Didn't you hear it?"

"We heard something," Kate said.

"Well, I can't hear anything with that damn music blasting in my ears." Matt put down his drink and walked over to where Dan was leaning against the juke-box.

"Excuse me, son."

Dan looked down at the sheriff, thought about it a second, and then graciously moved his two-hundred-and-thirty-pound frame.

Matt pulled the plug and the singing melted into a low blurb before fading completely. "Sorry, Willie." He looked at Dan and nodded his thanks before turning his attention back to George. "A UFO, huh?"

George nodded, obviously relieved that someone was finally taking him seriously. "I think it crash-landed about twelve miles due west of here."

"That would place it in the middle of Stan Farquil's farm," Matt surmised.

George nodded again and everyone began to listen.

Kate was still amused. "I can just see Stan's cynical old face when he sees little green men walking around his field."

The crowd chuckled, but Hal looked at her somberly. "It's possible," he said. "We shouldn't laugh. What if extraterrestrials were on Blackwell's Island right now, right at this moment? It's nothing to scoff at."

"Well, if there are any visitors here, they'd have to be out of their minds," Kate answered lightly. "It's off-season, you know. No one comes to this island in January. Not even extraterrestrials."

"You came here in January," the sheriff reminded her, and for some reason his words had a sobering effect. The mood in the bar seemed to shift, giving George an edge. Matt gave George a keen look. "A UFO, right?"

George nodded with absolute determination. "That's what I saw."

"And you're sure it wasn't a jet plane or a shooting star?"

"It was an unidentified flying object."

Matt nodded. "I believe you, George."

"You do?"

"Yes, I do. Now if you'll excuse me . . ." He turned back to the bar and lifted his drink to his lips. This time he was stopped by Kate, who grabbed his arm before his could take a sip.

"Shouldn't you investigate?" She was smiling, but she was also baiting him, and her fingers increased their pressure ever so slightly. His arm was sinewy and strong. She liked touching him, she realized distractedly.

He gazed at her hand on his arm. Then his eyes locked with hers. "It that an order?"

Kate actually had to turn her gaze away from that liquid-blue stare. "I— Well, it *is* your job," she said.

"What's that supposed to mean?" He was staring at her hand still holding onto his arm.

"You're a civil servant," she blurted out. "That means you work for me, for all of us."

"Hmmmmph!" Matt put down his drink and removed

her hand from his arm. "Okay, boss, what do you want me to do?"

Kate answered promptly. "Investigate, of course."

There was a hum of general agreement.

"I'll do that," Matt said. "First thing tomorrow morning. I'll drive out to Farquil's place and see who he's entertaining for breakfast."

"Why not right now?" She eyed him warily, but was unable to resist the urge to needle him. Not after all those times he'd been such a stickler for propriety. He was the sheriff, and it was his job to investigate odd happenings. So let him investigate.

"They could already be setting up their death rays," she added cheerfully. "If you hurry you can stop the invasion before it gets underway."

"Very funny."

"She's right, Sheriff." George Digger found his voice. "I know you think I'm crazy, but what if this is for real? Just consider that, will you? Maybe I'm right."

Matt took a drink and sighed. "Let me be sure I've got this straight. You want me to check out a possible UFO and make sure there isn't going to be an invasion. Is that it?"

Kate was shaking with suppressed laughter. "Face it," she said, "this island is strategically located." She made sure she had everyone's attention and then looked back at him. "Let's see, now. We've got National Air Defense headquarters for the northeast only twenty miles away on the mainland. I'd say that this airspace is a vital doorway to the United States, wouldn't you?"

No one disagreed with that. Every school child on Blackwell's Island knew it. The island had been a key to the mainland ever since the British had been handily rebuffed in 1778.

"It could be the Russians." Hal shook his head. "They'd love to strike at us first with an advanced force."

"That's possible," Kate mused, going along with him. "But the Russians don't have spaceships that sophisticated, do they?"

Matt looked at her bitterly. "Just what are you trying to do here, create a riot?"

Hal was not to be deterred. "Oh, they have 'em, all right. But they're not ready to use them, not yet." He frowned thoughtfully. "I say if something landed on Farquil's farm, it was either one of ours, or..." He stopped dramatically and gestured toward George. "Or it came from somewhere else."

The tavern erupted with loud conversation, and Kate was starting to enjoy herself. It was rare that something exciting happened in the middle of the winter. Leave it to Matthew Caine to spoil everyone's fun before it even got started. Determined to play this out to the hilt, she announced, "I don't think anyone should go out there unless they're properly armed." She reached up above the cash register and pulled down an antique rifle from the hooks it had been resting on for at least a hundred years. It wasn't loaded, of course, but only she knew that. She cocked the trigger with a loud snap, making Matt choke on his drink. "You never can be too careful."

"Give me that thing," he barked, slamming his glass down on the bar. He snatched it out of her hands and held it firmly. "This is getting ridiculous. UFOs! What next?" He gestured angrily at Kate, and the tip of the rifle knocked against his drink, causing half the contents to spill onto the bar.

She blinked at him with angelic innocence and

slapped down a rag. "Would you like a refill?" She could see that he was trying to keep his temper. His eyes met hers.

"I suppose you believe in little green men?"

Kate thought it over while everyone waited for her answer. Just having the sheriff in her territory, playing on her turf, was a heady experience. "Not necessarily. You know, they could look just like us."

"Who could?" Matt asked.

"Them," she said, pointing up at the sky. She made a sinister face. "The E.T.s."

That got Hal motivated. "Kate's right. They could infiltrate and we'd never know who they were."

"Don't be ridiculous. There is no 'they,'" Matt said. "Now will you all sit down and forget about this?"

"How can we?" George asked. "That thing is out there on Farquil's farm. You'll see it for yourself. All you have to do is drive out there."

Matt gave the man a long, hard look and shook his head. "What thing?"

Kate tapped him on the shoulder and waited for him to acknowledge her. When at last he slowly turned to face her, she could see that he was in no mood for games. "The thing that George saw landing on Farquil's farm."

"I think he said it crash-landed," Hal added. "Am I right, George? It crashed there?"

George shrugged. "It did something strange like it was turning nose-up and then coming bottom down." He used his hand to illustrate the maneuver; everyone was very impressed.

Florence Wilmot and her husband Roy were sitting at the corner table. She ran the needlepoint shop and he was the island attorney. "Well, if no one else is going, I am!" she announced, getting to her feet. "This sounds exciting and I'm not about to miss it. Come on, Roy. This is better than watching TV any day."

Her husband followed her and, after a moment, so did George and Hal. Dick Battering, the high school principal, spoke up just as they reached the door. "Maybe we should call Farquil."

That stopped everyone in their tracks. Something as sensible as that seemed to put a damper on the excitement. Kate could tell that every person in the place was eager to head out there, but Dick was right.

"Good idea," she said. "Let's call him."

Matt looked at Kate and gestured for her to bring him the phone, which she did readily.

Several seconds passed as everyone waited to hear what Stan Farquil would say. While they were all sitting in the bar talking about it, he could look right out his window and confirm or deny what George had said. Matt dialed, waited, disconnected, then dialed again. After another moment, he hung up and looked at her. "Phone's dead."

That bit of news was met with the incredible hum of voices all talking at once. The excitement rose again, and even Kate was beginning to be taken in by these bizarre events. "It was working ten minutes ago." She took the receiver from Matt, held it up to her ear, and frowned. "It's dead, all right. No dial tone."

Matt eyed her sarcastically. "Thank you for confirming that for me."

Hal ran over to the pay phone, and put a coin in, and dialed Stan Farquil. But he had the same result. "Dead," he repeated.

Then the worst thing that could happen, happened at

the worst possible time. The lights flashed on and off a few times before going permanently out.

No one spoke.

Hal walked over to the window while everyone waited for him to state what they all suspected.

"They're out everywhere down the street," he said matter-of-factly.

Jack Gardner confirmed the report from the opposite window. "Yup, they're out on this side, too."

"It's that thing," George said in a whisper.

Matt said crossly, "What thing?"

"That thing that landed. It's—it's stopping us from communicating."

That was all anyone needed to hear. Hal made a bee-line for the door, followed by practically everyone else in the room. "This I got to see."

George had whipped out his keys. "We'll take my pickup. If it's up in Farquil's hill, we might want to bring something back."

Matt could hardly stand it. "What do you mean, *bring something back?*"

George stammered, "You know, the—the thing."

"What *thing?*"

The room was back to a hush at these words. Kate tapped Matt's shoulder and he turned to look at her. "The thing," she said. "You know." She pointed skyward. "Our visitor from another planet."

That did it. In the next instant pandemonium broke out as everyone headed for the door.

"Let's get moving, before it gets away."

"I've got a fishing net in my trunk."

"We'll need plenty of rope."

"Hold it," Hal said, shrugging into his coat. He was the last to leave. "We'd better stop at my place. I got to get Sally." As cars were revved up and took off down the snow-filled road, Hal's voice could be heard calling after them. "I'll be with you as soon as I get Sally."

In the end only Flint, Matt, and Kate were left in the bar. None of them spoke for a full minute.

Kate lit a candle and put it on the bar next to Matt. She looked at him. He looked at her. A leaky faucet under the bar dripped noisily. Kate eyed it and, with a swift kick from her boot, pushed the lever shut. The water stopped dripping and all was deathly still.

Kate was the first to break the silence. "Who is Sally? Does Hal have a girl friend?"

"It's his shotgun," Matt said.

Flint grumbled. "Idiots!" Then he picked himself up and headed past the bar, giving Kate a forlorn look. He shook his head and marched slowly over to the stairs that led up to his small apartment.

Kate watched him until he was out of sight. "Well," she said with a small sigh, "that's that. If there are any little green men, I guess we'll be hearing about it soon enough." She busied herself wiping the bar, and stole a look at Matt. He was staring morosely into his drink. Kate had been a bartender long enough to know when someone was truly bothered by something. "Shouldn't you get out there?"

Matt shook his head without looking up. "I suppose I should. Last thing we need are those clowns shooting at each other in the dark."

CHAPTER
Two

THE SHOCK ABSORBERS in Matt's Jeep were virtually nonexistent; each bump in the icy road sent Kate clear off her seat. The Jeep also had no heat and she was glad she had worn an extra sweater under her parka.

"Why were you trying to get drunk tonight?" she asked directly.

He reached into his shirt pocket and tossed a folded telegram onto her lap. "It's this." Matt turned on the light so she could read it.

Kate unfolded it and read. Her eyes lit up and she broke into a broad grin. "Well, congratulations. You're going to be a grandfather!" She turned to face him. "When is the big day?"

He gave her a long, mean look.

"Oh, dear. I said the wrong thing, didn't I?"

Matt looked as if he had been sucking on a lemon.

"There is no 'right thing' to say, so I suggest you say nothing."

"That bad, huh?"

"I'm in a mean mood, Kate. Spare me the conventional wisdom."

She let him alone for several minutes during which he made terrible progress on the road. He managed to hit every bump and Kate was sure he was doing it on purpose. After a particularly jarring one, finding herself clutching the edge of the seat as she sank onto the floor, Kate decided to put a halt to it. She reached her foot across the floor and tapped the brakes. Matt hit the clutch immediately and allowed her to slow the Jeep to a complete stop.

She looked at him sternly. "Now look here. Maybe you want to die, but don't you think you should ask me if I want to go along for that kind of ride? I've got a whole new life ahead of me."

He met her look with one of baffled innocence. "Oh, right. Well, while we're on the subject, just what kind of a life is that, and where is it?"

She was surprised by his curiosity no matter how gruffly presented. He was in a mean mood, all right, but his interest was intriguing. "Why is that important to you?" she asked lightly.

He shrugged laconically. "Just curious."

"After three years you've suddenly taken an interest in me?"

He scowled, looking even more gruff than before, and she liked it. She had never been much of a teaser, but he seemed to be asking for it with both barrels.

Matt put the Jeep back in gear and this time he drove more sensibly. His voice took on the level coolness that had often infuriated her in the past. "Don't be so cocky.

I was curious, that's all. That FOR SALE sign in your window had everyone mumbling tonight." He threw her a glance that was clearly hopeful, and Kate hid a smile.

She pursed her lips and watched him out of the corner of her eye. He was fidgeting in his seat, and his hands changed position on the steering wheel three times. Apparently she was driving him crazy and this knowledge delighted her. To think that this strong, implacable, confident man was actually being affected by her. It was the first time she had ever seen him react so strongly to anything. He was obviously waiting for an answer and she took a deep breath. "But we haven't finished with you yet," she said sweetly. "I can't talk about my life when you're still so upset about yours. I'd like to hear the whole story."

"The whole story? What makes you think there's more?"

She laughed. "Mister, I've been a bartender for years. People use me as a psychiatrist, social worker, advice columnist, and all-around basic shoulder. So don't try to fool me. I'm too well trained. And, besides all that, you were throwing them down like a regular, back at the tavern."

Instead of answering her, he fished around in his pocket and came up with a photograph of a young woman. Kate snatched it from him and examined it. It didn't look like a new photo, but the light was too poor to guess when it had been taken.

"She's pretty. Your daughter?"

A look of genuine surprise crossed his face. "No," he said, quickly taking it back and pocketing it.

His foot leaned heavily on the accelerator.

"Well, what is your problem, Matt? I should think you would be happy at a time like this."

"You don't understand. I'm too young to be a—a grandfather!"

She let out a long "Ahhh", and nodded. "Now I get it. Suffering from the premature aging syndrome."

At those words, Matt sped up, hitting a huge bump that sent Kate flying toward the ceiling.

"Listen, Matt!" She was yelling. "If you can't control your feelings, at least control your speed."

He slowed down with obvious reluctance. "Sorry."

The Jeep jounced along. They passed quiet, snow-covered fields and occasional abandoned barns. Only the headlights told her they were still on anything that resembled a road. "That's better," she said, daring a long look at him. His profile was a little ragged. He needed a shave and there were hollows under his eyes, but he had the look of a man who had grappled with life and come to terms with it. She saw courage in his face, and a certain sense of victory. Only the intensity in his eyes betrayed his current distress.

The Jeep wasn't new or spotless, but it was orderly. A stack of magazines sat over the dashboard in front of her, and she picked one up. It was an old issue of *Field and Stream*, the cover featuring a hunter with a bow and arrow taking aggressive aim at a frightened deer.

Kate noticed that Matt's eyes darted at it for a second. "Does he get it?" she asked, pointing at the cover.

"Does who get what?" He squinted at the magazine, and laughed. "Oh, you mean the hunter."

"Yes."

He hesitated a second as if his mind was still on the other subject. "Uh, yeah, but not on the first arrow. The article is about tracking a wounded buck. The guy spent seven hours in the Adirondack Mountains looking for that animal in order to kill it. In the end he swore he'd never kill again. Following a blood trail from a wounded animal can really turn anyone off."

His eyes seemed to darken as he said that, and Kate's instincts were aroused. "You've done it, haven't you?"

He grinned. "Yeah, I'm an expert. And I've tracked more than just wounded animals. I even wrote a story about one that got published."

Kate was surprised. "*You* actually wrote a story— that got published? What was it, a true confession about tracking deer in the great backwoods? I can just imagine the title. *I Killed Bambi's Mother.*"

Kate's laughter was cut short as the Jeep bounced wildly for a long moment. It hit a slick ice patch and careened crazily, but Matt maneuvered it deftly into control. Kate let out her breath and cast him an admiring look. The man was unflappable—a quality she was only now learning to appreciate. The Jeep was now moving steadily along, and Matt continued talking as if nothing had happened. "It wasn't a deer," he said with deadly calm. "It was a lost child."

She sat up straight and stared at him.

"A seven-year-old kid named Charlie wandered away from his parents' car in the middle of Montana."

Kate could think of nothing to say, but the chill matter-of-factness in his tone told her that he wasn't exaggerating. If anything, she guessed that he was underplaying his story.

Matt eased up on the gas pedal while he continued. "It happened in late November. That can be a desolate time of year up there, especially for people like Charlie's parents, who were from New York. They were parked at one of those state forest rest stops for a few minutes. They thought their son was sleeping in the backseat, but they were wrong. They resumed driving

down the highway, unaware that their son was walking
around the middle of nowhere with just a security blanket and a bag of Gummi Bears. What made it worse was
that they didn't discover their mistake until two hundred
miles later."

He stopped talking as if to close the subject, but Kate
was hanging onto every word. "I didn't even know you
worked in Montana," she said.

"I didn't," he answered. "But when I heard about the
case in the news, I packed my gear and took the next
plane out there."

"Just like that?"

"Just like that."

She tried to imagine him putting all his gear together,
simply chucking everything else to go into the middle of
nowhere to help find a lost child. That was a side of him
she had never imagined.

"Are you surprised, Kate?"

"I don't know what I am. You're always so gruff and
disconcerting. You keep to yourself and never come
around the tavern. Now you're telling me this." She
turned sideways and gave him a long, cool once-over.
"You know, you ought to open up more. Be a little
friendlier."

"Is that what everyone in town says?"

Kate opened her mouth to say yes, and then closed it
again as she realized it wasn't true. *She* was the one
who thought so. Night after night, Kate heard all the
town gossip. But the truth was, hardly anyone ever
talked about Matt. They all knew him and they all re-
spected him. But the islanders were not gossipy and she
realized uneasily that he was the one person she knew
nothing about.

Still, she could see he was curious. She probed a

little further. "Do you care what people think?"

He didn't hesitate to answer. "Only when they're sober." He smiled broadly as if he knew he had one-upped her.

Kate smiled back. "Sometimes a little alcohol lets the truth out."

"Well, I'll just try that next time I need a suspect's confession." He laughed. "Yes, sir, that's just what I'll do." He glanced at her again, his direct gaze sweeping over her in a most unsettling way. "We'll just bend the law a bit. Next time I arrest someone, I'll bring him over to your bar instead of the jail. Then we'll just keep buying him drinks until he confesses to the crime. Heck, we can even move the courthouse over to your tavern. The judge can serve the drinks and all the witnesses will be required to down at least three stiff belts before swearing testimony."

"Well, that would be great for business." She studied him for a moment. "What ever happened to that lost boy?"

Matt shifted in his seat and changed the subject without much subtlety. "Tell you about it later. That's Farquil's farm just up ahead."

He turned the Jeep sharply and plowed up a hill on a smaller road. Lights twinkled just over the crest and Kate could make out the outline of a barn roof. Someone had placed a dozen flares along the road and it was easy to follow it up the rest of the way. There was something glowing even beyond that, but she couldn't make out what it was.

They arrived at a place in pandemonium. Cars were parked everywhere at crazy angles and people were running around with lanterns and flashlights. They all hailed the sheriff as if waiting for him to take charge.

Hal Freedy ran up first, Sally swinging at his side. "You've got to see it, Sheriff. It's a real honest-to-goodness flying saucer and it's parked right over there." He used Sally to gesture toward the field about a hundred yards behind the Farquil house.

Matt grabbed the barrel and took it away from Hal in order to check the safety pin. It wasn't on. At the top of a small hill about a hundred yards away, something was buried in the snow. It was glowing red-hot and a small fire was burning around part of it. People kept edging slowly toward it to get a better look but no one got too close, as if they were afraid it would explode.

Kate couldn't believe her eyes. "Well, I'll be damned. Looks like old George was right." She was staring in disbelief when Matt used Sally to let off a shot.

The blast made Kate jump, but it accomplished its purpose; it got everyone's attention.

"Now listen up, everyone," Matt called out. "I want you all to get back down here, away from that thing." He turned to Dan Shere, whose build was more than enough to scare anyone, extraterrestrial or otherwise. "Son, I'm deputizing you again."

Dan's face lit up. "You mean like last summer when we almost had those riots?"

Matt heaved a tolerant sigh and spoke firmly and distinctly. "A group of eight-year-olds throwing toilet paper at a tree is not what I'd call a riot. Now listen carefully. I want everyone behind my Jeep." He activated the safety latch on Sally and handed to Dan. "Hold this for a while. Don't use it—just hold it."

Kate followed Matt as he maneuvered the crowd back a safe distance. There must have been at least a hundred people there and each one seemed to have a different opinion. Even as they all walked backwards, more cars drove up. Kate was gratified to see that despite some intermittent grumbling, they all followed Matt's directions without question.

Matt watched as the newcomers jumped out of their cars without even bothering to shut off their headlights. "That's Blackwell's Island for you," he muttered. "We have no telephone service, but somehow everyone gets the news—fast."

Kate couldn't help laughing. Although whatever was up there on top of the hill was obviously of some consequence, the rest of the scenario was equally priceless.

Dan was using a bullhorn to order people back. Kate noted with amusement that no was listening. They were all edging forward again, almost against their own inclination, propelled by overwhelming curiosity.

Those with cameras kept trying to move in for a closer shot, while souvenir seekers were gathering up the odd chunks of still-warm metallic debris that littered the snow.

Kate stooped to examine one herself. After being satisfied that it was indeed broken metal and not some weird other-worldly substance, she tossed it aside.

The ship or whatever it was now glowed less than fifty yards away.

Every time Matt turned his back on the crowd, they'd inch closer. And each time Matt had to try again to control them.

"Get back, folks, please. This could be dangerous."

"You heard the sheriff," Dan Shere yelled into the bullhorn. "Now get back before you get hit by a laser."

At those words Matt did a double take and gazed sharply at his deputy. "Laser?"

But Dan's words worked. The idea of something ominous shooting lasers at them from the alien ship was enough to compel the most curious into doing an about-face and scurrying back down the hill.

Kate tried and failed to stifle a laugh until Matt caught her. His cold look stopped her mirth and she realized with a sudden flash that this situation could be more serious that she had thought.

Then it happened.

George Digger, who by now had edged his way back in front, suddenly stopped and pointed. "Something's moving out the top of that thing!"

As everyone watched in frozen awe, a long metal bar protruded out the side of the thing, unfolding slowly like an umbrella, and began to turn around. Kate found her hand automatically locking under Matt's arm.

"It's a death ray," Florence hissed to her husband, Roy, who stepped back and pulled his wife with him.

The rest of the crowd followed suit, increasing the distance between them and Matt and Kate, who were now standing alone as the most likely targets.

There was total silence as every eye was mesmerized by the revolving umbrella.

Kate couldn't bear the suspense any longer. "Matt, what do you suppose that is?" she asked. Her hand was firmly clutching his arm, and she realized that she felt much safer holding onto him like this. Matt was so naturally commanding that it seemed even aliens would stop and heed his words.

"Radar, maybe?" he guessed. "I've seen that sort of gadget when I was in the service."

Suddenly Dick Battering's voice boomed through the bullhorn, making everyone jump. "Do not be afraid. We will not harm you." He inched around the edge of the crowd, walking toward the thing and waving a white flag slowly up and down. "We will not harm you," he repeated.

Matt gave him a withering look and jerked his thumb in the direction of the crowd. "Get back there with the others, will you, Battering?"

"Be careful, Sheriff," someone warned. "I'd hate to see you turned into a pile of dust by a death ray."

Kate wasn't laughing anymore. That just wasn't funny.

Matt edged up the hill with Kate tagging along at his side. She refused to let go of his arm. She wasn't sure if he needed her as much as she needed him at that moment, but it didn't matter. She wanted a closer look, but there was no way she was going to attempt that by herself. Maybe Matt felt the same way. She had the feeling he did, and that a sort of unspoken partnership had formed between them. No one challenged her newfound status, fragile though it was.

Finally they stopped, only ten feet away from the mysterious object. It was a simple cylinder, lying half buried in the snow. A long fiery trail across the field revealed the path it must have taken as it hit the ground, finally sliding to a halt.

Matt drew a quick conclusion. He pointed at the burnt-out path. "That's some kind of fuel burning. I've seen plane crashes like this," he added. "This could go up."

"You mean explode?"

He turned and led her quickly back down, away from the danger.

"What *is* that thing?" Kate asked.

The whole town was waiting for Matt's answer, and he shrugged. "I've never seen anything quite like it. It sure as hell isn't one of ours."

Dick Battering wasted no time in marching forward again and waving his flag. Matt caught him out of the corner of his eye and pointed where the crowd had retreated. "Back," he ordered and, turning to Kate, added, "and you, too."

Kate was more than happy to obey. She walked back down the snowy path. She had forgotten to wear her boots and snow was squishing into her shoes and soaking the hems of her jeans. Now that she was away from the source of heat, she realized that it was freezing cold. She shivered and clamped her teeth together to keep them from chattering. She caught up with Dick, who continued waving his flag as he backed away.

At the bottom of the hill, Kate turned with everyone else and watched as Matt walked right up to the saucer. His face was lit against the light of the persistent flames as the umbrella continued to revolve only a few feet above his head.

"Now that's a brave man," George Digger said. "I'm gonna vote for him next election."

"If he's still alive," added Florence crisply.

"Be careful, Matt," Kate found herself calling out.

Matt waved down at her. "Hey, Dan—get me a crowbar from my Jeep."

"What for?" Dan asked. He looked decidedly uneasy.

"Never you mind what for. Just get it."

But Dan didn't budge from his spot.

"You okay, Dan?" George asked. "Dan?"

Kate acted on her own and went over to the Jeep. After rummaging through the trunk, she came back with the tool and placed it in Dan's hands. The huge man still wouldn't budge.

Matt grew impatient. "Let's have it, already. This thing's liable to go at any moment now."

Dan handed it over to George Digger. "You take it up there."

"Oh, no, not me," George said. "I'm not a deputy." He motioned to Hal Freedy, who moved away from him.

"Not me neither," Hal announced. "I saw *War of the Worlds*."

"You saw what?" Kate asked.

"The H. G. Wells movie. Remember the beginning where the three men get killed by the death ray?"

"Yeah, I saw that," Roy said. His face had turned a chalky white and he had backed away on his own, completely forgetting about his wife. The rest of the crowd followed suit.

Then something occurred to Kate. She looked quickly over the crowd. "Has anyone seen Stan Farquil?"

Murmurs went through the onlookers, but the answer came back negative.

"They must have got him," Hal called out. There was a hushed silence. "Poor Stan."

"Where's the crowbar?" Matt yelled. "Hurry it up, this thing is as hot as an oven."

In an instant, Kate grabbed it out of Dan's hand and ran blindly up the hill. She had no idea what inspired this rash act, but somehow she couldn't believe that anything really dangerous was going to happen as long as Matt was standing there. Matt snatched the crowbar from her and wasted no time. He immediately went to work on what appeared to be the door of the ship. "I've got to work fast if I'm going to rescue whatever is in there before this thing explodes."

Kate gasped. "You mean something is *alive* in there?"

The crowd reacted feverishly.

"There's a living thing in there!" came a voice from down the hill.

"The *thing*? Did they say *The Thing*?"

"Aliens!" Someone shouted it loud and clear and it sounded like a battle cry.

A little boy's voice broke through the chatter. "It's E.T., Daddy. E.T.! Don't worry, he's friendly."

Matt continued to work frantically on the door, but it was hard going. All Kate could do was stand petrified as the flames seemed to grow higher.

"The damn fuel is leaking too fast. I may not make it."

Kate realized what he was saying. The fire was well on its way to becoming a conflagration. She could see that Matt had gotten the crowbar jammed under the door hinges. "Jump on it hard, Matt," she cried. "Put your full weight on it."

Matt slammed his body hard against the bar and the door flew open. A sudden explosion followed, which sent Kate sprawling into the snow. Everything seemed to go fuzzy in her head after that. A huge fire flared up immediately and then there was another explosion that left her completely dazed. In a semi-coherent state, she thought she saw a distorted figure of Matt emerging from the door of the ship. And then there was a third explosion.

She blinked hard and looked up at the UFO. It was now surrounded by fierce flames that refused to die down in the snow. Someone was standing in the small doorway of the ship. "Matt? Is that you?" She stood up groggily and peered through the blaze as the strange figure became two, and then three.

She regained her footing and stood rooted to the spot, staring into the flames. She thought she heard

Matt calling something. There was another flare-up, followed by a series of short explosions. Suddenly Matt was tackling her to the ground. A huge explosion of deafening proportions sent a wall of fire up over the entire area. The tornado-like force was overwhelming. It sent Kate and Matt sprawling haplessly down the hill, tumbling crazily head over heel. When at last they stopped rolling, she was on top of Matt, cradled in his arms. They both looked up to see a large ball of fire spreading rapidly across the field.

CHAPTER
Three

THE PEOPLE BELOW were dumbstruck.

By now the ship was a total bonfire, fed by the fuel in its tanks.

Matt looked at Kate as they sat up in the snow, warmed by the blaze. She could see superficial burn marks on his face and hair. She reached out gingerly and touched his singed scalp. "You don't have to worry about any gray hairs for a while," she whispered. "They were all burnt off."

They helped each other up and surveyed the damage. The entire hill was blazing and littered with burning debris.

Deputy Dan came running up to them. "Are you all right, Sheriff?"

Matt growled, "Yeah, just terrific."

Dick came running over to join them. The top of his

flag had been seared off. "Did you see anyone in there, Sheriff?"

Matt didn't answer.

"Oh, come on, Sheriff. We heard you say something was in there."

George Digger's voice called out excitedly, "Look, there's Old Man Farquil." He was pointing to the barn; Stan Farquil was standing in front of it. The old farmer had a pitchfork in his hand, and was dressed in a bathrobe and a pair of rubber boots. He was obviously relieved to see them.

"It landed with a huge explosion," he explained groggily. "I was in the middle of closing up for the night when it knocked me unconscious." He rubbed his head and looked around. "Hell, looks like the whole damn town is here."

"Get him to the infirmary and have him checked out," Matt instructed Dan.

Everyone had crowded around Matt and Kate, and he groaned when he saw the expectant looks on their faces.

"I didn't see anything," he said. "Not a darn thing. Now why don't we all go home while the evening is still young. I'll get in touch with the proper authorities and have them investigate. It's probably just a satellite that went out of wack and exploded in our backyard. That's all."

No one appeared satisfied with that explanation. A few people shrugged and lingered around, waiting to get a closer view of whatever was still burning at the top of the hill. Others headed back to their cars, but didn't get in. Everyone stood around talking and many people were taking pictures. No one wanted to leave.

Dan prevented the very brave from getting too close. Most onlookers finally began to give up and head back to their cars. With the thermometer near zero, and the winds blowing up a new storm, the majority of the curiosity seekers vanished, leaving just Kate and Matt and a few stragglers.

Hal Freedy was jumping up and down in an attempt to stay warm as he talked to his buddies about heading back to the tavern for one more round. Their talk of aliens had been cooled considerably by the weather, and they now agreed that they had been quite foolish.

"I guess we really got carried away, didn't we, Sheriff?" George said as he fished for his car keys.

Roy shrugged. "Probably just a satellite, right?"

"Yeah, or a missile off-course. Maybe from that army base on the coast."

Matt agreed readily, almost too readily, Kate thought. "Absolutely. No question about it. Go home, fellas. We'll have the authorities take care of this. In the morning it will be all straightened out." He gave them all a reassuring smile, followed by a decisive glare aimed at Kate. She frowned uncooperatively and shook her head.

The men nodded and turned toward their cars, but Kate glared back at Matt and announced dizzily, "I think I saw them."

George Digger froze in his tracks and turned back to face her. "You what?"

Hal was opening his car door, but he slammed it at once when he heard her words, punctuating the night with the sound.

Jack Gardner just stared at her.

Matt laughed uneasily and tried to shoo them all away. "Go home, all of you. I'll check all this out tonight." He turned to Jack. "You still got that portable generator?"

Jack wasn't listening to Matt. He was still staring

open-mouthed at Kate. "You saw . . . *them*?

Matt tapped him on the shoulder. "Hey, Gardner, you hear me? Come on, Jack." The man stood motionless. "Earth to Jack. Earth to Jack. Oh, great, now look what you've done!" The last comment was addressed to Kate, who was frowning uncertainly.

"You saw what?" Jack asked Kate in a hushed, awe-struck tone.

Matt countered fast. "She saw what I saw, an explosion. Too close for comfort. Now, about that generator. Put in in my office tonight, okay?"

Jack finally snapped out of his stupor. "Yeah, sure."

"Okay, terrific," Matt said, trying to summon up his usual authority. "I'll call the coast as soon as possible and get the National Guard out here. We'll have them send over some help. Meanwhile let's all go home."

None of the men moved. They were staring out across the snowy moonlit meadow.

"Could they be out there?" Hal asked.

"Only one way to fine out," Jack said.

Matt was thumping his hand impatiently against his thigh. "So go ahead out there and get a better look," he said. "I won't stop you." He gave them all a sardonic smile. "But you'll be wasting your time."

None of them moved.

"Go on," Matt said. "What are you afraid of?"

The men didn't answer, but they all turned slowly and began to make their way back to their cars.

Matt called out one last order to them. "I want that radio hooked up and working tonight." He stood with his hands on his hips as the cars backed away, one by one. When he was sure they were gone, he turned to Kate, who was standing quietly in the snow.

The fire was dying out, sharply diminishing the quality of light, and Kate became aware of the moon for the first time. The sudden chilly silence was beautiful, and she shivered suddenly as Matt approached.

"I'm sorry," she said softly. "I shouldn't have said that, right?"

Matt shook his head. "News like that will spread across this island like a forest fire. I won't be able to control it. Anything could happen. You've seen how people react to a thing like this." He rubbed his forehead wearily. I'll bet that in less than an hour they'll be organizing posses back at your bar."

Kate was crestfallen. "I should have known. I'm really sorry, Matt. I think the force of that blast made me a little woozy."

He put his hands on her shoulders and looked down at her, causing a little chill to run through her. "Are you all right?"

"I think so." She stood gazing up at him, and his hands remained on her shoulders, feeling firm and warm. Something passed between them, something invisible and yet almost tangible in its intensity. The stirrings of the rapport she had felt earlier had suddenly blossomed. She and Matt were a team. They stared at each other for a long, weighted moment. "I'd better get back," she whispered.

"Take care of yourself."

She nodded wordlessly. The cold air caused their breath to come out in wisps, but she didn't feel the cold. Staring up at Matt's roughened, hardy face, she realized with a sudden, shattering clarity that she was deeply attracted to him. Why hadn't she been aware of it before?

"If I'm right in my prediction," he said, "you'll have your hands full tonight."

She managed a smile. "So will you. But at least it will be good for business. No one is going to get much sleep tonight."

"Give me a few more minutes, and then I'll take you back to town. I just want to check on a few things." At last his hands dropped from her shoulders, and she shivered again. Her eyes followed his lean, muscular form as he headed back to where the ship was still burning. It was now mostly a red glow of embers and pieces that were strewn around.

Not wanting to be more than a few feet from him, Kate trotted up after him. In the glow of the ship he had resumed his customary air of command. He looked around at the debris, but there was nothing moving and nothing unusual. Kate felt foolish suddenly, struck by the newfound knowledge of her feelings toward him .

"Well," she said, trying to sound chipper, "let me know if you need any help." Matt was busy poking through the debris, and he walked around to the other side of what had been the ship. "Not that a hunk like you needs any help," she mumbled to herself.

He squatted down for a moment to examine something and then looked up at her with the trace of a grin on his face. "Did you mean that?" he asked.

"What, about needing any help?"

He turned to look back at the embers. "Never mind."

Matt continued exploring the site for another twenty minutes, during which Kate tried to stay warm by moving close as possible to the dying embers of the exploded ship. Eventually, however, she began to grow numb from the cold, and wondered how Matt could tolerate it without a sign of discomfort. The man was intractable when he wanted to be.

She began to stamp her feet to keep her circulation moving, and watched Matt as he studied something with his flashlight.

Finally she called out to him. "Hey, what do you say we call it a night before I turn into an icicle?"

Matt looked back at her and waved a hand. "I'll be with you in a few minutes. Why don't you go back to the Jeep and warm it up? The keys are in the ignition."

"Now that is an excellent idea." She quickly turned and ran down the hill. The Jeep was sitting where Matt had left it, its door wide open. Kate approached it with a puzzled frown and ducked inside, anticipating warmth at last; she discovered the keys were missing. Letting out a frustrated sigh, she banged the dashboard and looked back up the hill. "They're not here," she shouted. "You must have them. Check your pockets."

He didn't answer.

"Matt?" She waited, but still no answer. She heaved a breath. "Here we go again." And with that, she headed once more up the hill. This time there was no Matt, either.

Kate was in no mood for this. It was dark and late, she was freezing, and she was all alone in what felt like the middle of nowhere. "Matt? Are you out there?"

She looked across the ghostly field with the white snow glistening in the reflection of a full moon. Perhaps he was crouched down in a hole nearby and couldn't hear her. A sudden blast of cold wind made her tremble violently. She suddenly became inexplicably afraid. She waited anxiously for Matt to answer, but only the wind sang through the trees. Kate took a deep breath and counted to ten.

"Matt? Don't do this to me!" She thought she heard

footsteps behind her, and called out in a thin voice, "Matt? Is that you?"

She didn't like this at all, and her sixth sense told her to get out of there, and fast. A sudden movement out of the corner of her eye made her almost jump out of her boots. Something darted behind a group of evergreens. Kate wasn't sure if she was shivering from the cold or from fear. "I'm asking nicely," she called out, trying to sound calm. "Can we please leave now?"

His voice came from behind, matter-of-fact and calm. "All set, let's go."

Kate whipped around and looked at him in disbelief. Her gaze volleyed back and forth between the evergreens and Matt, and she forced a weak laugh. "Okay, Houdini, how did you pull that off?"

"Pull what off?" Matt looked impatient, as if there was nothing on his mind except a peaceful drive home.

Kate looked at him quizzically. "You know. How did you go from those evergreens over there to standing right behind me without a helicopter?"

But Matt had no idea what she was talking about, and he didn't seem particularly interested in finding out. He marched past her and headed down the hill. "Let's get out of here, I'm freezing."

She watched him leave, but she hesitated before following. She was still a little dazed from what had just happened. "First he's over there, then he's here," she said aloud.

The moon had disappeared behind a cloud, making the once-glistening snow a dark, cold, forboding mass. Kate could barely see in front of her face. The evergreen branches over her head shook a little, and although she attributed it to the wind, her imagination began to torment her. "It must be the darkness," she whispered to herself. "That's it. I didn't see anything at all."

Matt's voice came from halfway down the hillside. "Come on, let's get moving. I'm freezing."

The moon came out once more, and the figure of Matt was easily seen heading down to the Jeep. Kate felt very vulnerable standing all alone at the top of the hill, but she didn't move. "I know I saw something," she said to herself. She walked with caution over to the evergreens to have a closer look around. There was nothing to see.

Matt grew impatient. "Hey, Kate. Let's get going."

Suddenly something fell right out of the trees. It crashed down through the branches and fell with a thud a few feet from where she stood. It could have been a pile of snow loosened by the wind, but Kate didn't hang around to investigate. In that moment she took off in a bolt, and in the next instant found herself running down past Matt, beating him to the Jeep. She was all out of breath as she dove inside.

"Having fun?" he asked.

She gave him a nervous look. "Something tried to pounce on me from the trees," she said.

Matt raised a brow. "Pounce? You mean, like a lion?"

She nodded her head.

"I think the wind has been playing with your imagination," Matt said dryly. "Take it from an expert camper—it can do that to you. And I should know. I once saw a man run away from his own shadow, thinking it was a bear. " He started chuckling to himself. "It was the funniest sight I'd ever seen."

Kate looked at him as he laughed, and realized that he may be right. Between the cold and the strange events of the evening, her mind was tired and susceptible to flights of fancy. "I guess I am a little jumpy," she admitted. "You're probably right. It must have been my shadow that fell out of that tree back up there."

He laughed again and she joined in, trying to sound more confident than she felt. But she noticed that Matt was regarding her with open amusement, genuinely wanting to share a good joke, and her fear vanished when she caught the sparkle in his eyes. It was amazing how her view of him had changed so drastically, but now that it had, she was sure it was never going to go back to its former distance. Had he somehow grown more youthful, or had she simply gotten older? And did it really matter?

Kate spoke up without even thinking. "How about coming over to the tavern for a nightcap and finishing that story about the lost boy?"

"Can I take a raincheck on that one?" he asked. "I've got a small crisis on my hands at the moment." He smiled in a way that made her catch her breath. "Maybe some other time, okay?"

"Okay," she whispered. "I have a feeling I'll be open very late."

"We'll see, okay?" He reached for the keys in the ignition, but his fingers touched air. "Do you have the keys?"

Kate was surprised. "I thought maybe you did."

Matt let out a sigh. "That idiot Dan probably has them." He leaned his head back on the headrest and groaned loudly. "Terrific," he said. "This is just great."

He reached for the microphone of his CB, but dropped his hand in frustration when he realized that he needed to turn on the car to make it work.

"Now what do we do?" he asked, his annoyance obviously mounting.

"Ah—we could—well . . ." Kate pointed to Stan Farquil's house. "Under the circumstances I'm sure he won't mind." Without waiting for an answer, she jumped out of the Jeep and headed up to the house. Matt came up behind her, the beam from the flashlight dancing ahead of him.

Farquil's house had retained quite a lot of heat despite the fact that the electricity was off. After being exposed to the cold air for so long, Kate actually felt hot as soon as they stepped inside. Matt flashed his light on the thermostat in the hallway which registered a comfortable sixty-eight degrees. "That won't last long," he said as he looked around. "I'll light a fire. You find some candles."

He handed her his flashlight and she found her way toward the kitchen. On the way she stopped to look at photos in the hall of the Farquil family and realized that the grandchildren had left the island. Stan Farquil's wife was dead and he lived all alone here. Kate had seen him quite often at her bar, but she had never been inside his house. She wondered if Matt's place was like this. Now that she thought about it, she wasn't even sure where it was. She had been on this island for three years and there was some simple things she still didn't know. While she rummaged the kitchen for candles and another flashlight, she could hear Matt stacking logs next to the fireplace and she called out to him.

"Stan Farquil sure has a large family."

She heard Matt grunt something that sounded affirmative.

"Did you know his children?"

Another grunt was followed by a short explanation. "I went to school with Stan, Jr."

Kate let that rummage around in her mind for a while. Practically everyone on this island had a history here. Everyone except her. She found a bunch of candles in a drawer, but her curiosity had been piqued and she decided to go exploring for a few minutes. The house seemed very large for just one person. Farquil must get lonely, she thought. So many lonely people on this island, but no one ever talked about it.

She traveled upstairs and peeked into four bedrooms that were filled with sturdy maple furniture, hooked rugs, and the discarded trappings of adolescence. The rooms were all in order as if Stan was waiting for his children and grandchildren to visit. It was easy to tell which room was which. Twenty-year-old toys lay neatly on shelves and in closets, waiting for the eager hands of the grandchildren. It was a lovely thought and Kate paused, witnessing three generations of a family in one glance.

There was one more room at the end of the hall and she went toward it curiously. The knob turned easily in her hand and she looked inside. There was nothing but a large table in the middle of the room and she groped for the light before remembering that it was out. As her flashlight danced over the room, a broad smile spread over her face. This was a billiard table, the cue sticks and billiard balls waiting to be used. There was a dart board on the wall and all sorts of games lining the shelves. In the far corner next to the window was a small wet bar with three stools in front of it. But the bar looked as if it hadn't been used in a long time. The Farquils must have entertained here once, but no longer. Bottles of liquor lined the shelf below the window and she checked the inventory as if it were her own tavern. She called down the stairs to Matt.

"Hey!"

"Hey, yourself." He was still sounding a little gruff, but Kate realized that she was getting used to that. It didn't mean he was irritated—necessarily. It was just how he sounded.

She was determined to have a good evening and she kept her voice light and inviting. "Come on up here. I want to show you something."

There was a long silence and then she heard his footsteps as he came down the hall and up the stairs. She met him on the landing and led him down to the game room.

She walked over, picked up a cue stick, and turned to look at him.

Matt leaned against the door frame and smiled at a sudden memory. "I used to play with Stan here—oh, a long time ago," he said.

Kate fingered the cue stick. "Care to play again?"

He grunted, but followed it with a smile and a nod. "It's hard to play without any light."

"I think we can fix that," she said, brushing past him. She headed back into the kitchen and returned with two dozen candles.

"Aha," Matt said, getting into the spirit. "Wait right here." Not to be outdone, he went into the kitchen himself and returned with a box of silver foil.

"Okay, you've get me there," Kate said. "Just what are you going to do with all that silver foil?"

"It's an old camping trick" he explained. "I'm going to get ten times as much light out of all these candles."

Kate was still skeptical, but she had learned to take him at his word. "I'll believe it when I see it."

CHAPTER
Four

FIFTEEN MINUTES LATER, all twenty-four candles were burning, brightly reflecting light onto the table from the silver foil backdrop. The room was as bright as sunlight, but the mood was much more interesting.

Kate smiled and decided she liked it. She examined one of the creations, impressed. "It really gives off a lot of light," she exclaimed. "Where did you learn to do this?"

"I took a series of survival courses a long time ago. Add to that twenty years as a hunter, camper, and all-around outdoorsman, and you score a lot of points in the experience department."

"In short, you're an expert."

Matt made another monosyllabic sound and Kate hid a smile. She realized that he was actually modest about his accomplishments, and his lack of macho strutting was immensely appealing. He was confident of his abil-

47

ities, but didn't need to shout them from the rooftops.

Matt reached for a cue. "I'll break first," he announced. Placing the cue at the edge of the pool table, he lined up a shot. "The number three ball, corner pocket," he said, pointing to the red ball on the outside of the pack. With a whack, he sent the white cue ball smashing hard against the fifteen balls at the end of the table. The balls flew in all directions, and Kate watched in awe as the three ball dropped into the corner pocket.

Matt now had a huge grin on his face.

Kate was impressed. "I never saw anyone make that shot before." She gave him what she hoped was a sportsmanlike look of admiration. "You really are full of surprises, aren't you?"

He banked another ball into the middle pocket and then another and another. Kate was beginning to get the picture that this wasn't going to be a give-and-take game, and she relaxed, leaning against the wall. As Matt lined up a very difficult shot, Kate remembered the half-finished tale of the lost boy and decided to bring it up.

"What's to tell?" he answered with a shrug. "I had just gotten back from doing two years in the army. I heard about it on the news." He gestured randomly and sent the white cue ball heading down the table. It missed the target completely.

Kate arched an eyebrow and moved forward, tapping her cue with one finger. "You hear about a lost boy and suddenly you're packed and off and running to Montana? Just like that?"

"Just like that." Matt leaned on his cue and continued. "There was already a search party in progress when I arrived. There were about a thousand National Guardsmen and police in all, including five helicopters and ten track dogs, plus a journalist from the Guard who hung around talking about golf most of the time."

"But you're the one who found him," she persisted. "How?"

"If you want to catch a fox, you have to think like one. I know kids," Matt said in his no-nonsense way. "I also started out from the last place the boy was seen. Everyone else went tromping into the forest in the standardized pattern search."

Kate leaned against the table and listened intently. Matt was downplaying his role in the rescue, but he had a knack for explaining things. She became even more impressed by his knowledge of the outdoors. "So you actually followed his breadcrumbs, so to speak?"

Matt nodded. "That's a good way of putting it. I found him on the night of the third day," he explained. "He was huddled up inside a small cave, freezing, hungry, and scared out of his wits. The look on his face when he saw me was worth the trip."

Kate almost melted. She looked at Matt's face, intelligent, stubborn, a little careworn, and suddenly she wanted to wrap her arms around him and kiss him with all the warmth within her. It had been a very long time since she had felt that way about anyone, but the years of loneliness dissolved as she looked at him. But she couldn't carry out her impulse. Not here, not now.

She shifted slightly in an attempt to conceal her emotions, and concentrated on lining up her shot. She was gratified when the ball went rolling neatly into the pocket with a little clump.

Walking around the table and standing right next to him, she readied her next shot. He was standing very close and made no effort to move away. After sinking her second shot as well as the next, she straightened up and turned, and found herself looking right into his eyes.

Before she knew what she was doing, she reached up quickly and kissed him on the cheek.

"What was that for?" he asked, looking genuinely surprised.

It was too late to be embarrassed, so Kate blurted out the truth. "That was for rushing out to Montana," she explained.

Matt didn't say a word. Kate blinked nervously. There was nothing to do but go back to the game.

She leaned against the table and steadied herself for another shot. But she didn't take it. Instead, she stood back up, marched back over to Matt, and kissed him again on the other cheek.

Matt didn't react, but he didn't appear to be unhappy, either. Kate didn't care.

"And that was for saving that boy's life. What you did was incredible."

"Was it?"

"Yes, it was." She studied him in the flickering candlelight. "It was an enormous feat."

Matt seemed to struggle for a moment, and then he said, simply, "Thank you." She nodded a little, still staring at him.

His gaze became clearer and more penetrating, and somehow the balance of assertion between them changed. Kate looked down for a moment and Matt took a step forward. "Now that I've told you about that little adventure," he said, "how about you telling me one of your own?"

"One of my adventures?" Kate asked. "Like what?"

"Well, for starters, how about telling me about the

time you drove an open motorboat over the frigid ocean from the mainland to Blackwell's Island in the dead of winter?"

"That—that wasn't really an adventure. I was running away."

"Obviously. All the same, it must have been close to zero degrees out on the ocean, and the windchill would have been enough to keep the staunchest sailor curled up in bed for the day. It was an enormous feat," he finished, deliberately echoing her own words about him.

Kate barely knew what to say. "Thank you," she said at last with a concerted smile. A long silence passed before she bent down to take her shot.

But Matt wasn't finished. "Only a idiot or a desperate person with nothing to lose would drive a motorboat out here in the dead of winter." His voice became more commanding, assuming the tone she knew so well, and he dropped his cue to the floor with a decisive clunk. "I've always wanted to ask you about that. Which were you, an idiot or desperate soul?"

"Both," she answered without looking up, and with that, she sent the cue ball crashing successfully against its neighbor, driving it hard into the corner pocket.

But Matt wasn't going to let up. "Something must have happened to make you risk your life like that."

"A lot of somethings," she agreed. She turned around to look at him. As he waited with maddening patience for her to continue, Kate started to speak and then stopped. She truly did not know what to say.

She started again, and stopped again. There wasn't going to be an easy way to do this. She hadn't talked to anyone about this since coming to the island, and she felt that if the dam were finally opened, she would not be able to stop.

She closed her eyes and opened them again. Matt was still standing there, still waiting, but she caught a flicker of compassion in his eyes that broke her. Looking up at the ceiling and then staring straight ahead at the wall beyond him, she took a deep breath and let him have it straight. It was the only way she could say it. "In less than one year I managed to fall in love with the wrong guy, get myself pregnant, lose my teaching job, get ostracized by my neighbors, and end up before the state supreme court."

Matt digested this bombshell without any outward surprise. He nodded a little, smiled encouragingly, and said, "Want to talk about it?"

Kate had to think about that before answering. "No," she said finally, more harshly than she had intended. She didn't look at him. Instead, she turned back to the game, and missed her shot completely. Several seconds passed as she stood there, leaning on the table. Matt's presence behind her was almost overwhelming.

"I think you do," he said to her back. "After spending three years bottled up at that tavern listening to everyone else's problems, I think you do want to talk about it."

"Do I?"

"Yes. As a matter of fact, I believe that you've entertained fantasies of being on the other side of that bar of yours, sitting on a stool, sipping a martini, and pouring your heart out to the bartender. I'm right, aren't I?"

"Not about the martini," she said, mustering back some wit. "When it comes to the hard stuff, I'm for straight scotch." But she didn't want to turn around and let him see her face. It had to be a dead giveaway. Instead she groped to turn the conversation away from herself. "What about you?" she asked. "Tell me something personal about you. After all, why should I suddenly want to open up to a perfect stranger?"

He sounded almost annoyed. "Perfect stranger? Me?"

She turned around and faced him. "I can't even remember the last time you and I had a conversation before tonight."

Matt reminded her readily. "It was the night back in October when Grady Zeeny drove his car through your front door because you refused to serve him a drink."

Kate couldn't help laughing. Grady's pickup had ended up parked in the middle of the tavern. Luckily no one was hurt, but the place had been badly wrecked. There she had stood, forlornly surveying the damage when Matt came through what had once been the front door. She never forgot that look on his face or what he did next.

There was the sheriff, standing complacently and looking around at the mess as if it were something he had seen a thousand times before. As nonchalantly as he could be, he walked up to Grady's truck, rested his foot on the front fender, and proceeded to write him out a parking ticket. And just as cooly as he had come in, Matt placed the ticket under Grady's wiper, and walked out again without saying a word.

Kate shook her head at him. "Now that I recall, you and I never said a word to each other that night."

Matt thought that over. "Fair enough," he said. "What about this past August when I closed you down for a full weekend? I'm sure you can recall *that* conversation."

"I sure can," Kate said. Her anger rose at the memory. "Do you know how close you came to having a bottle smashed over your head?"

Matt didn't laugh. "As I recall, there were already quite a few bottles broken on heads that night."

She shrugged it off nonchalantly. "A quiet, civilized little brawl. I could have handled it myself. I didn't need you and that Neanderthal deputy of yours interfering."

Suddenly Matt burst out laughing.

"What's so funny?"

"What's funny is you on top of that table with a badminton racket in your hand thinking you could stop those five gorillas from beating each other's brains out."

Kate grinned. "I did hold them at bay pretty well, don't you think?"

"No," Matt answered seriously again. "In fact, I should have let them tear your place apart. It would have served you right."

That put a hard edge on the conversation, and Kate almost groaned when she remembered how she had been behaving. She moved away from him and gave him a deliberate once-over while formulating an equally bold question. "You haven't liked me very much since I came here three years ago, have you?" Her tone was extremely cool, but Matt didn't flinch.

He also didn't say a word.

"What's the matter?" Kate asked. If he thought he could take her down that easily, he would find out how wrong he was. True, she had run away and, true, she had been hiding out like a wounded deer, but even wounded deer have survival instincts, and right now hers were coming on strong.

Matt looked at her, picked up his cue, and went back to the pool table and lined up a shot. He didn't take it right away, nor did he say anything. Kate felt the air thicken with tension.

He was about to take his shot when Kate suddenly took it upon herself to put her hand on his cue and stop him cold.

He gave a sidelong glance that managed to be intimidating and sexy at the same time. "It's kind of hard to take a shot with you leaning on my cue."

She nodded. "It's kind of hard to play at all with a perfect stranger. Especially a stranger who has been around town for as long as you have. Now fair is fair. I told you something about me. Now it's your turn."

Matt gazed at her for a long time, his eyes penetrating hers. She felt breathless and time seemed to stop for a moment as he captured her eyes with his. Finally he broke the ice. He leaned on the table with one hand and kept that devastating gaze fixed on her face. Finally, as if having given it a lot of thought, he began to talk.

"I'm forty-one, and a widower with two daughters, ages twenty and eighteen." He said it so suddenly and it was so out-of-thin-air that Kate was instantly subdued. "The younger one is in college and the older one is married—"

"—and pregnant," Kate said, nodding.

"Ummm," Matt grumbled. He gave her a hard look, reminding her that he was still not comfortable with that information, and she smiled.

"Have you lived here all your life?"

"Yes. Except when I went to college."

"Oh. You went to college?"

"Yeah."

"Where was that?"

Matt finally took the shot he had been lining up for the past few minutes. He watched the ball drop in the hole before turning to answer. "Boston University. I've got a B.A. in sociology."

Kate's eyebrows rose and Matt caught the look. "You're surprised that I'm educated?"

She said nothing.

He looked at her steadily. "I'll bet you think that all I do is read *Field and Stream* magazine. Am I right?"

He was right. She couldn't deny it. A small flicker of a smile edged out from the corner of her mouth, giving her away.

Matt looked at her triumphantly. "I thought so."

"I guess I'm not the expert on people I thought I was," she said, attempting to concede gracefully.

"That's your whole trouble, Kate Brody. Like I was telling you before, you've been on the wrong side of that bar for too long. You're an excellent listener, and in most people that's a good quality, but in you it's an overgrown one, to say the least."

Kate shot back to get him off the subject. "We were talking about you," she reminded him. "In particular, why you don't like me."

"We were talking about us. Only I'm more up front than you and more trusting. Besides, I never said I didn't like you. You did." He let that all sink in and easily made another shot. By now there were only a few balls left on the pool table and he was winning. "You've been living here three years, Kate, but all anyone knows about you is that you can serve a good drink. You're Kate, the tavern owner."

"And you're Matt, the sheriff."

He looked sad when she said that. "You're wrong there. Or at least partially wrong. I wasn't always this reclusive. Everyone knows me on this island. I had a lot of close friends. Still do, in a way."

"I already know that," Kate injected. "George Digger and his gang say you used to pal around with them. From what I understand, there was that infamous Thursday night poker game at the tavern every week. And you even did an eleven-year stint as scoutmaster. And all those goofy practical jokes. I heard about what you and Freedy did to George Digger on Halloween five years ago."

He let out a chuckle. "George isn't still sore at me, is he?"

She laughed along with him. "No," she said. "George gets a kick out of it himself. He still talks about it, and he embellishes it more each time."

She let that roll around for a second and added, "What happened? From what I've heard, you used to be everybody's best friend."

He looked away and his face took on an ineffable sadness that went straight to her heart. Memories seemed to push their way up from beneath the surface, and suddenly he was lost in thought.

Kate watched him with growing understanding and a growing sense of control. She put on her barroom face. "Want to talk about it?"

Matt snapped out of it at once. "No," he said. "Not yet, that is." He gave her a hard look. "You see what just happened? You turned things around. You want me to talk? Well, what about you?"

"What about me?"

Triumphant silence was his only answer.

Kate said nothing. She was waiting for him to say something, anything. But Matt wasn't giving in. There were a few balls left on the table, but he didn't play them. Instead he threw his cue down and walked to the side. To Kate's surprise, he began blowing out the candles one by one.

The room began to grow darker.

And the darker it got, the more the walls around Kate seemed to open up. Suddenly she wanted to say something. Not to hear his story, but to tell hers. Suddenly she wanted to blurt the whole thing out, all the things she had never said to anyone. And it didn't make any sense. Matt wasn't an older brother or a father figure, or even just a friend. He was a very virile man to whom she was undeniably attracted.

Then it dawned on her that maybe that's why she had stayed away from him all these years with such purpose. Deep down she must have known how she could feel about him, if she let herself. But she hadn't wanted to let herself. She had very much needed all that time to herself, but suddenly, miraculously, that time seemed to be over.

She walked casually over to Farquil's little bar and sat down on one of the stools.

Matt took the hint. Taking a candle with him, he walked to the other side of the bar and placed it down so that it profiled their faces.

"What'll it be, stranger?" he asked.

"Scotch," she said. "Straight up."

Matt examined the stock and lifted out a bottle of Johnny Walker Red. He started filling her glass. "Say when."

Kate stopped him when it was filled halfway. She took a little sip. It had been a long time since she had had a drink. She made it a rule never to imbibe while working. Now it felt fantastic to be on the other side for once. The sense of freedom was even more intoxicating than the liquor.

"Do you mind if I bend your ear a little, bartender?"

Matt looked down the bar one way, and then the other. "It's pretty slow tonight. I guess I can take a few minutes to listen."

He leaned his elbows on the bar and gave her his undivided attention.

"What's on your mind, stranger?"

Kate considered where to begin. There was no question she'd been hiding out on this island after that one bitter year. Now, suddenly, it was time to get back to the real world.

But there was more to that. This island wasn't the real world, not for her. Getting back to the real world meant leaving, having the courage to meet someone new and start a new relationship. She did not have illusions about where this was supposed to lead. Marriage. Children. And she knew she wanted that. All of it.

But this island had not proved a good place to meet a prospective husband. Even her newfound feelings for Matt were just that—new. Maybe they were just a signal that she was ready, nothing more. After all, she couldn't throw herself at the first available man who came along. And she wasn't about to reveal all of this to Matt or anybody.

But she did want to talk about what had happened to her. The memories were now overflowing and if she didn't talk it over—tell someone, anyone—she knew she would crash.

Matt stood there on the receiving end waiting patiently. "Would you like to finish that drink first?"

"No, I don't need it."

He eyed her in disbelief.

With a shrug, Kate picked up her glass and gulped it all down. It had an immediate effect on her head. It was as if it softened her up and allowed her to open locked doors in her brain. And all at once it all came back to her as neatly as if it had been yesterday.

CHAPTER
Five

JOHN FLETCHER—or Mr. Wizard to his students—had been secretly dating her for half a year. He was fun and sexy and unpredictable. No one at the school where they both taught knew that they were seeing each other. They never looked twice at each other during school hours and when brought together for a school program or function, they never let on that there was anything more between them than a lesson plan. Kate knew that knowledge of their relationship among the students was an open invitation to prolonged gossip. It was bad for the school, and equally bad for her career.

If she and John had been married, of course, that would have been different. But at the end of a year she wasn't married. She was, however, pregnant.

When she told John, his attitude was cool at first, then angry. His solution was simple. Get rid of the evidence, and fast. Christmas break would be an ideal time to do it. No one would ever know.

At first she had agreed, reluctantly. But something happened to her before the winter break. John grew colder to her as the weeks passed and she grew warmer to the idea of the baby that was hers. The warmer she got, the further John drifted from her.

In the end, John dropped her. But that was only the beginning. As the winter gave way to warmer weather, Kate began to grow.

She could see herself standing in front of her class teaching. Although large-boned, she had a very slim figure. She had always favored knit dresses and she liked to tie a belt or scarf around her waist to add color and discreetly show off her figure. This style had attracted many an admiring glance and she had always liked it.

Her students liked her, too, and after awhile the scarves around her waist became a part of her school image. When at last she had to stop wearing them and take to loose-fitting, formless dresses, people simply thought she was putting on weight.

The students figured it out before anyone else in the school did. And because nothing official had been said, they whispered about it behind her back. But she knew that they had caught on and that it was just a matter of time.

It drove John, everyone's favorite teacher, crazy. He began to confront her in the hall, presumably to work out a study hall schedule, but really to hiss at her that she was crazy and stupid and a fool for trying to pull it off. He told her she looked ridiculous and managed to hurt her every time he saw her.

Whatever made her think she could go on with her

career and still live a normal life while having a baby quickly went sour when she was called into the principal's office for a nice little talk. The question was put to her, and she answered truthfully. She was fired immediately.

Matt poured her another half glass of scotch.

"Couldn't they just give you maternity leave?" he asked innocently. "That's what we do here at the Blackwell public schools. Why, just last year, Nancy Fielding had a baby. She teaches English at the high school. Heck, I'll bet you could have substituted for her until she came back. It took forever to find a replacement for her." Matt continued talking, expanding on the idea that Kate could teach right here on the island along with running a tavern. She knew that he was allowing her to collect herself, giving her time. "And unlike those dolts where you came from," he finished, "we folks have no problem with the high school English teacher being a part-time bartender."

"How about being pregnant and unmarried?" Kate asked quietly, but she couldn't keep the bitterness out of her voice.

That stopped Matt cold. He thought it over for a few minutes while Kate waited with a sinking heart.

"You took too long to answer," she said finally.

"Now hold on a second," Matt said. "You're not being fair here. I was thinking that I could see how it might create a problem, not that I didn't approve."

But it really was too late. Kate was starting to close up again. "That's just what I knew you'd say. That's what everyone said. That is, everyone but the ACLU."

Matt was surprised. "What does the American Civil Liberties Union have to do with it?"

Kate now addressed him as if he was the enemy.

"There are laws against discrimination in this country. Or don't you know that?"

Matt shook his head. "And you felt you were discriminated against?"

"Pregnant women have rights."

He nodded thoughtfully. "Yes. But then why is there so much controversy about abortion?"

"What does that have to do with it?"

"It means that some people see the pregnant woman and the baby as two different entities, with different sets of rights. I'm not saying I agree with them, just that I can understand why this issue is such a bombshell."

She studied him for a long moment. "Yeah, well. Some people also think that only *married* pregnant women have rights."

"What do you think?"

"Isn't that obvious? I wanted to have the baby, not get rid of it. That should have made the hard-liners happy. But I also wanted to keep on working. Hell, how did they expect me to support the baby if I didn't have a job? In short, I really didn't think it was anyone else's business."

Matt nodded, watching her the whole time. "That's you, all right."

"What do you mean?"

"You do outrageous things and think that no one is supposed to notice."

"They can notice." She shrugged. "But that's all." She managed a smile and took a long sip. "Do you think I'm being too hard?"

"Hard? Oh, no, that's the last thing you are. I think you're naive."

"What?" Kate was infuriated. "And all this time I've fancied myself a pretty cool character. I thought being a bartender was about the coolest thing there was to be. In charge; but aloof." She laughed a little wildly; the scotch was getting to her. "Do you mean to tell me that everyone knows I'm a fake?"

"Don't worry," he said, giving her a cheerful grin. "Your secret is safe with me. Everyone else on the island figures you've got a past, but that it's yours to keep, if that's the way you want it."

Kate settled down again, but her feathers were still ruffled. "I still don't think I'm *naive*. That's going too far."

Matt shrugged. "Didn't you realize that some people might have a problem with having an unwed mother teaching their kids?"

Kate eyed him shrewdly. "Would you?"

"No." He answered quickly and without pretense, and she knew he meant it. "But some people would, that's all."

"That's not what the state supreme court said."

Matt's face fell. "What?"

"I sued the school board and I won," Kate announced cooly, savoring what she knew was her trump card.

"Won?" He seemed to have trouble with that.

"Yes," she said. "I won. There was a big cash settlement. Lots of money. Not that it could ever be enough for everything I went through. It was, however, enough to buy Flint's tavern."

She was hardly rejoicing when she recounted all of this. There was more, and she could tell he knew it. By the time she'd finished her second glass of scotch, her nerves had calmed down considerably.

Matt seemed to ease back a little himself. "I think I remember reading about this in the papers some years back. But there was something else as well." He thought it over, drew a blank, and shrugged. "Well, anyway. It must have been hell for you in that town. The gossip, the newspaper stories, television coverage . . ."

"The full catastrophe," Kate agreed. "Everywhere I went, whether it was the grocery store, shopping for clothes, putting gas in the car—just driving around was hell. People talked behind my back. Some of them did it in front of my face. Others elaborately ignored me. I was the scarlet woman. The enemy of the people, the flag, and apple pie."

Matt was about to fill her glass again, but she put her hand over it to stop him.

"So what about Mr. Wizard?" he asked. "What was he doing all this time?"

"He got married and quit teaching right in the middle of the spring term. Moved south and ran his wife's family business."

"I hope you were glad you got rid of the creep," Matt said.

"I was," Kate agreed. "But then he showed up over the summer, out of the blue. He was all smiles and good wishes. And you know why?" She stopped for a second, reached for the bottle, and splashed another inch of scotch into her glass. She took a long swallow before she continued. "Because he wanted the baby, that's why. Turns out his wife can't have children. He went to court to gain custody, claiming that he would be able to provide a more stable environment for the child."

Kate let all that bounce around inside Matt's brain while she finished her drink. She was in no mood to continue. The scotch had made her tired and groggy, but it had anesthetized her temporarily from the pain of that year. She got up and called it a night. "I'm going to bed. Good night."

"Good night, Kate."

She left Matt standing there, and headed silently to one of the children's bedrooms where the toys lined the shelves. The temperature was already dropping, but there were plenty of blankets. In no time at all she was lying comfortably under the weight of several quilts, listening to the wind outside her window.

Although she was exhausted, she couldn't fall asleep right away. A new feeling was starting to sweep over her, and after a while she recognized it as relief. After all this time, it was wonderful to be able to tell her story to someone. How funny that of all people it should turn out to be a stranger like the sheriff. He had received her story the way he received everything, without judgment or even much of a reaction. And yet she was positive he understood. He was as solid as a rock, and just as dependable.

She thought back to his story of finding the lost child, and she couldn't get over it. She pictured him quietly and methodically packing and going to the airport without even telling anyone. Just showing up in the middle of a crisis and taking action.

The phrase "all alone" kept repeating itself in her mind. It was one thing to be lonely, but to be all alone and as capable as he was—that was exciting.

She had done something just as exciting, but also very foolish. Her thoughts returned to that day on the mainland on the frigid February morning when she had stood at the docks, staring across the ocean at the hazy outline of Blackwell's Island off on the horizon. With her suitcase sitting in the bow of the boat, all she could remember was the hum of the outboard motor, and her eyes glued to the horizon.

It was almost a three-hour ride, but it felt like an eternity. The waves weren't bad that day, but by the time she had made it to the harbor, the fingers of her right hand steering the boat were completely numb.

And there, standing on the docks, ever-present pipe in mouth, and seamed face peering sternly at hers was Old Flint. He had helped her out and onto the marina.

But Matt had been there also. He, too, was quiet and his face was equally stern. She remembered looking at him apathetically. He was standing near his patrol car, his hands in his pockets, just staring at her.

He never said a word to her. But later on, after she had warmed up, he came by to drop off her suitcase. He stood in the doorway of the tavern, suitcase in hand, while she sat with her back to him finishing off a bowl of hot chowder.

"You forgot this," he said.

He put it down right there near the door, and without another word, walked out.

That was the last thing he said to her for a whole year. Even when she saw him in town, he'd return her greetings with just a grunt or a nod.

Then she bought the tavern and, just as suddenly, he had a lot to say to her. All of it bad. Within two years of her purchase he had slapped her with fines for parking and noise pollution, warnings after the occasional brawls, or just plain nuisance lectures.

She never gave Matt Caine much thought, but now she was thinking about him in a startling new way, and she couldn't stop. Why had he been so reticent? She had heard tales of the pranks he used to be involved in, just one of the guys—until his wife died. Then he had apparently bottled up.

She would have liked to have known the old Matt Caine. He must have been a lot of fun. She'd have to ask him about that some time. She just couldn't imagine him doing anything deliberately hilarious.

She turned over and pulled the quilts up higher, determined to get a good night's sleep, when she heard the door begin to creak slowly open. Peering over to the hazy light produced by a candle in the hallway, she made out the silhouette of Matt's frame in the doorway. Only he appeared much smaller than his six-foot frame. He seemed to be only four-feet high. Kate had to blink a few times to make sure she wasn't dreaming.

"Matt?" she called out, but the figure didn't move. "What do you want?"

She was met with more silence. He just stood there without moving. Kate began to panic. Something was desperately wrong here. She felt the beginnings of a scream rising up from deep within her. One thing was for sure. Whoever it was . . . whatever it was . . . it was not Matt.

Kate was paralyzed. She was totally helpless, lying in a strange bed, staring at this . . . creature.

What had been intended as a scream came choking out as a low whisper.

"Matt!"

The thing in the doorway studied her with great curiosity.

She called a little louder. "Matt!"

Just as slowly as it had entered, the creature carefully closed the door and disappeared, leaving Kate shaking uncontrollably. And then she found her voice.

"Matt! Help! Get in here fast! Maaaaaaaaatt!"

The door crashed open and Matt Caine stood there with a blanket wrapped around his shoulders. He ran to the bed, but before he could ask what happened, Kate found herself throwing her arms around him and holding on for dear life.

He patted her back and held her warmly. "I guess you really needed to talk to someone about all that, huh? You know, you can't go around with that much hurting inside and not let go." He gave her another consoling squeeze and continued to hold her very close. "Well, I'm still here, so you just go right ahead and let it all out."

She almost did that, forgetting for a second what had brought him in here in the first place. With a big shove, she wriggled from his embrace and gave him an odd look. "No—that's not it. And stop looking at me with that concerned expression. You're not my father."

He gave her a look that was most definitely not paternal, and laughed. "I certainly hope not, for both our sakes."

Kate up and pointed at the door. "I saw it."

"It?"

"The spaceman, the creature from the UFO. It was here in my room."

She half expected Matt to continue laughing at her. Instead he assumed his sheriff personality. "Was it short, about four feet?"

Kate was surprised. "You saw it, too?"

"No," he said. "But I found tracks out in the snow on top of the hill. There were a lot of them. They must be short by the looks of the bootprints."

"There are a lot of them?" Kate clutched her blanket. "We're surrounded." She lunged for Matt's shoulders and threw her arms around him. "What are we going to do?"

She could feel Matt shrug. "Do?" he asked. "Why, we're going to go to sleep. But first I'm going to lock all the doors and windows."

He tried to get up, but Kate wouldn't let go.

Matt laughed. "It's going to be quite difficult for me to walk with you bear-hugging me to death." He took her hands and slowly removed them from his body.

"I'm going with you," she insisted. "I don't want to be alone for the rest of the night."

He thought that over, and smiled. "Do you mean that?"

"Yes. We can stay downstairs where there's a fireplace. I'll feel safer there."

"Fair enough. We really should sleep under the same blanket for maximum warmth. The temperature inside the house will be down to fifty degrees by morning."

Kate hesitated, and then nodded. If there was any man who could be trusted to do the proper thing, it was Matthew Caine.

"Let's go," he said.

Kate clutched her own blanket around her and followed him down the stairs. They found the front door standing wide open, and Matt pointed out the footprints in the snow. One set showed the creature, whatever it was, entering, and another showed it leaving.

Kate was awed but relieved. "Well, at least it's not in the house anymore." Still not satisfied, she secured every window in the house and made Matt set up several makeshift alarms just in case anything tried to enter again. All this took the better part of an hour, since Kate refused to leave Matt's side.

When at last they were finished, she stood watching

nervously as he set up a makeshift bed with a stack of blankets directly in front of the living room fireplace. Every time the wind blew up or a branch knocked against a windowpane, she jumped. Looking for something to calm her nerves, she knelt in front of the hearth and built up the fire until there was a substantial blaze.

By the time they crawled into the blankets, the room was glowing with a wonderfully warm fire. Kate comforted herself with the knowledge that strings stretched across both the front and back doors, with tin cans tied to them as an elaborate alarm system.

Matt tested one out before retiring. It rattled noisily, and Kate nodded.

"That ought to do it," he said proudly. "I used this same alarm out in grizzly bear country. One rattle and I was up with a flashlight in one hand and a gun in the other."

As he talked, he held the flashlight in one hand and produced his revolver in the other. He aimed it at the doorway. "Bam, bam, bam," he said, mocking her. "Down goes one dead alien."

Kate wasn't amused. "That's really not funny, Matt. How do you explain those footprints? Something is out there, and you know it."

He didn't answer and she settled down under the blankets suspiciously. After a moment Matt joined her. They lay side by side, almost touching but not quite, and Kate sighed. Matt sighed. She turned her head to look at him. "I mean it, Matt. And don't try anything funny, either."

"What on earth do you mean?"

"I mean like setting off one of those alarms on purpose as some kind of sick joke."

"Who, me?" The look on his face gave him away,

and she sat up and pointed at him accusingly.

"Aha! So I was right! I heard about you. George told me you used to be the biggest prankster on the island. You were really going to scare me, weren't you?"

"Well, you could use a little lightening up."

Kate sat up and said beseechingly, "I'm serious, Matt. This is no joke. I *saw* those things come out of that spaceship. I saw one right here in the house. Please, no jokes, okay?"

"Okay, okay." He took her elbow and gently made her lie back down. The sense of intimate comradery was beginning to overwhelm her. They were lying in a makeshift bed together, in a strange house in the middle of the night. "You're awfully jumpy about this," he observed as she struggled to pretend that he wasn't as close to her as he was.

"What bothers me is that you aren't," she retorted. "Why is that?"

"I don't worry about things until it's time to worry." With that answer, he turned away from her, onto his side, and nestled his head on the pillow to go to sleep.

Kate looked at him and decided that the best thing to do was to follow suit. She closed her eyes and tried to go to sleep, but her heart was still beating rapidly; she was all too aware of Matt's masculine presence only inches away. He was breathing deeply and she assumed he was already asleep.

Finally she settled down and, little by little, she began to drift off.

Just before she was asleep, Matt spoke softly. "Kate?"

"Ummmm?"

"What happened to your baby?"

Her eyes opened.

"Was it a boy or a girl?"

"A girl."

He said nothing more, but all at once his arm swung over her and rested comfortably across her chest.

"Good night, Kate."

"Good night, Matt." She closed her eyes again, feeling as if she had just docked in a safe harbor after a long storm.

CHAPTER
Six

IT WAS SATURDAY morning. Kate was awakened by the sound of a roaring car engine. Matt appeared to be dead asleep, a motionless hump under the mound of blankets next to her. She lifted her head from his shoulder and looked around. The sun was just coming up, the light filtering through the living room drapes. Surprisingly, it was quite comfortable in the Farquil house, considering that the heat was turned off.

"You'd think we'd wake up freezing," Kate said, suspecting that Matt was more awake under those blankets than he was letting on.

He grumbled something incoherently. "Did you say something?"

"I was just commenting on the amount of heat in this place. Maybe the electricity is back on."

Matt's head appeared as he pushed the blankets down. Without even opening his eyes, he threw an arm out over the rug. He groped around blindly for a few seconds before wrapping his fingers around a log that had been lined up in front of the hearth. Kate watched in amazement as he tossed it sight unseen at the fireplace. It landed atop the smouldering heap of embers, scattering white clouds of debris every which way. A moment later it was burning peacefully.

Kate was impressed. "Have you been feeding that fire all night?"

"Mmm-hmmm," he mumbled.

She was impressed and could think of nothing to say except for a very sincere, "Thank you."

Outside, the engine continued to rev up and down as if someone were trying to warm it up. The horn beeped a few times as the motor roared.

Matt finally roused himself, bringing himself reluctantly to his feet. "That must be Danny. He probably wondered why we didn't show up back at my office last night. He was probably too scared to come out here in the dark looking for us."

"I don't blame him," Kate said. "After what I saw in my room . . ." She was interrupted by the insistent honking of a car horn.

"All right, already!" Matt yelled. "I'm coming!"

The horn kept up incessantly and Matt grew annoyed. "What the hell is the matter with that guy?"

"I'll run out and tell him we're all right," she volunteered. "He's probably afraid to come inside the house."

She grabbed her coat and went outside, running down to the front driveway. Although it was very cold, there was no wind and the sun felt warm on her face. When she got to Matt's Jeep, there was no sight of his deputy.

"What is this, hide and seek?" She looked around in

a circle, her eyes coming back to the Jeep. Something was very wrong. She glanced around again. There was no sign of another car. Her eyes slowly turned back to the Jeep, and what it was doing.

"Oh, my God, it's on!"

Sure enough, the keys were back in the ignition and Matt's Jeep was purring rhythmically. Kate stared at it hypnotically, and then put a hand to her mouth in disbelief. After a brief moment, she cautiously stepped backward, moving away from it. She hadn't gone far when she bumped up against Matt. Only she didn't know it was Matt.

The scream she let out was louder than the car horn had been. And she jumped high enough to punch Matt in the chin with her head. When she regained her breath and found her tongue, she let him have it. "Don't you ever sneak up on me like that again! Do you understand me? You scared the life out of me!"

Matt paid her no heed. His eyes looked past her at the keys in the ignition. He examined the snow around the door.

Kate followed his somber glance. "Footprints," she said, calming down.

Sure enough, tiny bootprints led up to the Jeep and then away again. Matt bent down and examined them closely.

"These little fellas must have taken my keys last night."

That was enough to send Kate's overworked imagination into overdrive. "Do you think they did it on purpose to keep us here last night?"

"Could be." Matt squatted down in the snow, still looking at the prints. "They're about four-feet tall, I'd say. I think I can easily take on a four-foot creature from another planet. Nothing to be afraid of, right?" He glanced sideways at Kate as if testing her.

She gave him an innocent look. "Who said anything about being afraid? Did I?"

He actually laughed at her. It was the first time he had smiled that morning and she liked it. It eased her tension a little.

"Now, not a word of this to anyone," he said. "We don't want to launch a full-scale riot just yet, do we?"

Kate didn't see the reason for so much secrecy, especially when something out of the ordinary was clearly going on, but she didn't want to argue with him. She wanted to get out of there, so she nodded briefly.

"Good." Matt stood up and came over to her. "Are you hungry?"

She nodded. "Starving. But I'd like to eat in town, if you don't mind. I don't like being alone out here with those . . . creatures still lurking around."

They cleaned up Farquil's house, hopped in the Jeep and headed back out on the road to the harbor. Along the way they encountered a group of eight telephone poles that had obviously been razed by the crashing ship. But that was only the beginning.

As they drove along what was usually a quiet, desolate road, they encountered a number of highly unusual sights. The first was stretched across the road outside Rudy Mason's cottage.

Matt stopped the Jeep just in time, skidding to a halt only inches from it.

He let out an unbelievable huff. "Is that what I think it is?"

Kate was just as astonished. "It's a fishing net, isn't it?"

Sure enough, stretched across the road was a huge

thirty-by-thirty foot fishing net. A cottage window opened quickly, and a young man stuck his head out. He had a shotgun pointed right at Matt. "Who goes there?"

Matt gave him an angry look, but Rudy was beaming. He seemed to be very glad to see them.

"Matt! You're alive!"

"Darn right I am. But I won't be for long if you don't put that damn fool gun away."

"Sorry, Sheriff, but you can't be too careful, you know." He called out to his wife. "Okay, Martha, let them through." Kate noted that he didn't look sorry at all. He appeared to be enjoying himself immensely.

Mrs. Mason came running out to greet them. As she untied the net, she looked around uneasily at the landscape. "Everyone thought they got you."

Kate was glad for an ally, and spoke up without thinking. "They almost did. They took our car keys. That's why we were stuck out there. I actually saw one last night. I was never so scared in all my life. It came right at me—" She was about to continue her narration when a direct command from Matt cut her off.

"Stop it, Kate. Put a lid on it. Now." He spoke quietly but emphatically. It was nothing less than a command, but she obeyed.

But it was too late. The look on Martha Mason's face told Kate that it wouldn't be long now. Soon that little tidbit of news would have the whole island up in arms.

As they drove past Mason's booby traps, Matt had only one thing to say to Kate. "Congratulations, big mouth. Now we're in for it."

He was absolutely right. Kate looked back at the Mason cottage, and saw Rudy and Martha already jumping into their car.

Matt saw them through his rearview mirror. "There

they go. By this afternoon your little piece of news will be wagging on every tongue on this island."

Kate was chagrined. "Would an apology help any?"

Matt just shook his head. "Don't worry about it." He drove on silently, and Kate stole a look at him, wondering if he thought she was a perfect idiot. She hadn't meant to blurt out so much, but she had to tell someone, and Matt hadn't seemed very receptive to her qualms. He seemed to think the whole thing was nothing more than a silly nuisance.

Matt looked calm and controlled, as always. He was now sporting a day-old beard, but this made him look rugged instead of messy. She reflected that he had kept them warm all through the night by keeping the fire going, and she had to admit, as usual, that his common sense and practicality came in handy.

As they pulled into town, Kate realized that they hadn't spoken a word during the entire ride. Matt appeared to be deep in thought.

"I'll have to take a rain check on that breakfast, if you don't mind," he said as he pulled up in front of the tavern.

"Not even some coffee?"

He shook his head. "Priority one is to get in touch with the mainland before this thing gets out of hand. I'll be busy all day just getting the electricity back up."

Kate nodded gingerly, not wanting to be reminded of her transgression. "Well, how about dinner tonight?" she asked.

"Maybe. Let's see what happens."

She stood on the sidewalk and watched as he sped off down the street to his office. She knew that by late afternoon the cars would be parked three deep, and an unofficial town meeting would be held at her place.

It all came to pass as she knew it would. It didn't take long for the Masons to drive all around the island with the news, and by late afternoon the tavern was crammed with people. Kate's only help was Beatrice, her part-time waitress, and Flint, who did the cooking back in the kitchen.

The fireplace was kept busy all day, filling the crowded room with a cozy, woodsy smell. The beer flowed continually, and even the limited menu was strained to its limits. Kate had to run over to Digger's store to replenish her bread supply, but estimated that she'd be fine until new supplies were flown in at the end of the week. The phones were still down and, as far as she knew, no one had contacted the mainland.

Matt had been so busy that she hadn't seen him all day.

"I heard he's been in his office all day talking to the authorities on the radio," Hal Freedy said as he elbowed his way to the bar, which was packed three rows deep. He had on his white pharmacist's jacket under his coat. He reached out and Kate put a mug of beer in his hand. "So tell us already," he asked Kate. "What did they look like?"

Everyone nodded excitedly and pressed forward to hear.

Roy Wilmot was sitting at a table by the door with his wife Florence, who held her knitting. He called out to the crowd, "Forget it, guys. She's got orders not to talk about it."

"Orders? Orders from whom?"

"Yeah, and why not? What's the big secret?"

"We have a right to know!"

"Is it an invasion?"

But Kate kept her mouth shut. "Sorry, everyone. The sheriff will tell you when he's ready."

"You saw them, Kate." It was Rudy Mason. His wife was by his side. He had on an army jacket with live ammo attached to a belt around his waist. A knife in a sheath hung from the belt as well.

Kate looked him up and down and shook her head. "I don't think you'll be needing that knife," she said.

He almost pounced on her. "Why not? Is it because they have ray guns?" The crowd began speculating and talking all at once and Kate looked around, amazed at the way every little thing was blown out of proportion. Matt was right. She shook her head, determined not to say another word, and the crowd groaned. "Awww, come on," they pleaded.

"Sorry, everyone, but Matt gave orders."

"Where is Matt, anyway? You'd think he'd have brought in the army by now."

Again, the place buzzed with questions, but a new voice silenced them.

"There's no reason to panic, everyone." It was Dick Battering, the high school principal. Kate was surprised and grateful to hear him say this, but his next words made her close her eyes and groan. He jumped up on a table and proceeded to make a speech. "What we need to do is communicate with these creatures. They're probably as scared of us as we are of them."

"Don't be too sure," someone shouted. "Wasn't Kate attacked by one?"

Kate was flabbergasted. "Attacked! Who said I was attacked? I just said that I saw one of them in my bedroom at Farquil's place."

"They took your car keys." It was Roy Wilmot. He

looked at everyone and repeated it for effect. "They took her car keys."

Everyone began talking.

"But they gave them back," Kate added. She was getting knee-deep into the subject she had sworn to avoid. But it was hard not to. "They were probably just curious," she finished weakly.

"They wanted to keep you out there," Hal Freedy suggested. "Maybe they wanted to examine your bodies?"

"Or take them over," Dan Shere's voice interjected. The large deputy was standing by the jukebox, and everyone turned to look at him. "Remember that movie, *Invasion of the Body Snatchers*? That's just what they did."

Hal Freedy nixed that idea. "Naw, that's too far-fetched."

Kate was relieved to hear this tiny bit of common sense, but Hal didn't stop there. "Maybe they were in the back of the Jeep when Matt and Kate drove back this morning. Maybe they got out in town and they're roaming around right now, outside this very tavern."

Everyone looked around, suddenly suspicious.

Hal pointed an accusing finger at Kate. "You let them in."

"Ridiculous!" Flint was standing at the corner of the bar listening and, after handing Beatrice a tray of food, he growled at them. "You're all a bunch of idiots. That's what I think." He turned his back on them and marched into the kitchen, letting the door swing shut behind him.

The place was silent for a few seconds. Kate took the opportunity to try once more to reason with them.

"I think we should accept the fact that whoever they

are, they're cold, hungry, and by now very tired. They may also be very frightened."

Just then the door to the tavern opened and a blast of cold air gusted through, sending a shiver through Kate. But it didn't close and she looked up to see Matt standing in the doorway. He was looking around, his eyes finally coming to rest on Kate. She smiled, heartened to see him, but he was all business.

Pushing through behind him came Jack Gardner, followed by George Digger and his wife Mary Ann. George looked upset.

"They were down in my cellar," he announced.

This produced a mild pandemonium as the volume of voices in the room rose and then dropped. Everyone waited with baited breath.

George continued. "The place is a mess. Looks like a cyclone hit it. The produce is all over the floor. You'd think they hadn't eaten in days."

Hal Freedy jumped on this news. He pointed at Kate once more. "What did I tell you? You and Matt probably drove them into town without knowing it."

Matt looked at him as if he had lost his mind. He walked up to the bar, stood right in front of Kate, and turned around to face the population. "Now there's no need for panic," he said. "They haven't attacked anyone. All they did is steal some food."

The place was silent as everyone thought about this. Kate noted to herself that he was finally admitting to the town that there were indeed some pretty strange visitors on the island.

"Well, at least they're not hungry anymore," Matt said. "Just tired, cold, and perhaps a little scared."

"They're not tired anymore either," Mary Ann Digger said. Her voice was actually shaking, and Kate frowned. She knew Matt wanted this to be conducted in a low-key manner. Mary Ann looked around fearfully, as if she were afraid someone was eavesdropping.

George interceded. "They've been sleeping down in my cellar the whole day."

"Ever since Kate and Matt drove them into town," Hal Freedy said.

Matt whipped around and gazed at Freedy, who was nodding importantly. "Now listen up, everyone," Matt said in his I'm-the-authority voice. "I want you to shut off your imaginations for a while and get the facts straight." He gave Kate a sidelong glance when he said this, but he didn't look accusing. He looked like he was asking for her help. His confidence in her made her straighten up and listen with respect. "There are creatures walking around this island, true, but they haven't hurt anyone, and they haven't given any indication that they intend to."

"Not yet," someone shouted, producing an audible hum of reactions throughout the tavern.

Matt waited patiently, dragging his hand across his eyes. "Now you may all be wondering why the authorities haven't arrived yet." He hesitated, thought for a moment about how to proceed. "Well, uh, the problem is that my radio is on the fritz."

Everyone reacted.

"If any of you has a ham radio, I'd greatly appreciate it if you could bring it over to my office. We can hook it up to my generator."

Kate beamed. "Grady Zeeny has one." She went to the phone and began to dial before realizing it didn't work.

Matt turned to Dan Shere. "Get out to Zeeny's and see if he can bring it in to me." He turned back to the crowd. "If we have to, we'll send someone by boat to the mainland tomorrow for help. Meanwhile, I want everyone to stay home and stay warm."

No one moved.

Roy Wilmot spoke up. "This is the warmest place on the island, Sheriff."

"And the safest," someone added.

Matt grunted. "Fine, terrific, stay all night if you like." He held up a hand. "But do not attempt to find these creatures. Do I make myself clear?" Like school children being lectured, everyone nodded emphatically. Kate knew that it was useless. These people were primed and ready to go out hunting for aliens no matter what.

"Is that it, Sheriff?" Hal Freedy asked.

Matt looked at him hard, as if searching for trouble, but answered him evenly. "Yeah, that's it. We have no phones, it's getting dark, and I'm cold, hungry and tired. That's it." He was about to leave when he suddenly seemed to remember something. He looked at Kate. "I want to see you as soon as possible in my office." He didn't look happy when he said it, and Kate shrank back.

"Is it something I did or said?" she asked nervously.

"Asap," he said. With that he left as abruptly as he had entered.

Kate had never been in Matt's office. She had walked by it a thousand times, but had never been inside. It was close to seven o'clock when she was finally able to get away from her tavern. It was the best business day she had ever had. The food had gone as quickly as the beer, and by the time she left, her food supply had dwindled to a couple of steaks, some frozen fish filets, and some cans of vegetables.

Matt had called her an hour before she arrived to ask her to bring him a ham and cheese on rye. She didn't have any more ham or cheese, and besides, she thought he deserved something more after working so hard all day.

After turning the tavern over to Flint for the evening, she went to her room and changed into a brilliant blue knit dress and a pair of leather boots. The dress was ladylike but showed off all of her curves. She also put on some lipstick and some mascara, dusted her cheeks with a little blush, and took her hair out of its ever-present crescent-shaped barrette. It fell into smooth waves around her shoulders. Looking at herself in the mirror, she realized with a pang that this was the first time she had dressed up for a man in a very long time. She was well aware that her appearance was much too dressy for Blackwell's Island in the middle of winter. The locals, men and women alike, favored sturdy out-door gear during the off-season. But, she reasoned, Matt had probably never seen her in a dress. And she wanted him to. Tonight was the time to start, whether he was ready or not.

She showed up at Matt's office, leaning a heavy tray of food against the door. "Hey in there—open up! Your food is getting cold."

The door opened quickly, and Matt hurried back to whatever it was he had been preoccupied with all day. He didn't notice the tray of food or anything else. Kate shoved the door closed with her foot.

An old-fashioned oil lamp on Matt's desk was the only source of light. He was busily working on what appeared to be the radio.

"It's as warm as toast in here," she said by way of greeting. She noticed a wood stove burning in the corner. Next to it was a small gas generator, which obviously had enough power to drive the wood stove. Matt was hunched over the radio, but when the aroma from the hot food reached him, he finally looked up.

"Well, well, what's this?" he asked with an appreciative grin. "What's the matter, all out of ham?" He laughed at his own joke and gestured behind him to the single jail cell. "Do me a favor and put it on the table in there."

She peered doubtfully into the gloom. "In the cell?"

"That's right."

She went to the cell, and kicked at the door. It opened with a creaky sound on its hinges. She managed to find the table, and after lighting a small candle she was able to see clearly. What she saw was a big surprise.

There were two beds protruding from the wall at right angles to each other, hanging from metal chains. The table was in front of the small window, large enough to allow two people to eat comfortably. She put the tray down and looked around, bemused. There was a picture of the harbor painted by a local artist hanging on the wall, and silk flowers were arranged in a vase on a shelf, next to a few framed photographs. She recognized his daughter. Next to that was another picture of a woman.

"You sleep here," she surmised with some surprise.

He looked at her. "It's my home away from home. My place in town, if you will."

It was cozy, but rather solitary, she thought. "You must get very lonely."

"The only thing I get is hungry. And right now I'm starving. I've been working on this radio all afternoon." He rolled his chair away from the desk. In the flickering light from the lantern, he looked like a sheriff from a bygone era. He had shaved, and he was wearing a leather vest over a plaid shirt.

Kate walked over to him. "Please don't be angry with me."

"Angry?" He shrugged. "Why should I be?"

"You shouldn't," she said firmly. "But why did you want to see me? It sounded pretty important."

"It was." She thought she detected a twinkle in his eyes. "I thought I'd take you up on that offer for dinner."

Kate barely concealed her surprise. She was positive she'd been in for another lecture. She summoned a feminine smile and decided that this was definitely the right moment to take off her coat.

If Matt had been reticent, critical, or bossy in the past, he was none of those things now. Kate realized with vast amusement and a distinct sense of feminine power that he looked exactly like a fifteen-year-old on his first date. She slipped the heavy wool coat from her shoulders and let it drop onto a chair. Shaking her hair around her face, she gave him a winsome smile.

"Uh—well, well," he said, looking utterly nonplussed. "That's a very—uh, that is you look very nice."

"Thank you," she said graciously. She sauntered back into the cell, presumably so that she could check on the food, but really so that he could get a full view of the dress. When she returned, feeling deliciously in control, her gaze fell on the file cabinets set up in five rows along the wall.

She did a double take at the floor where they stood. It was littered with a huge, messy mound of paper. Two chairs were overturned behind them, a coatrack lay broken in the corner, and a stapler and a tape dispenser sat in a pile of paper clips. "This place looks like a cyclone hit it," she said with growing apprehension. She stepped forward to get a better look. What appeared to be a pool of black ink had spread into a small river on its way out the back door. Little feet had obviously stepped in it, and the frenzied pattern of black footprints zigzagged away from it.

She looked up at him, her forehead creasing with this new worry. "They were here, weren't they?"

CHAPTER
Seven

MATT NODDED. "You should have seen it before I cleaned it up." He pointed at the radio. "They smashed it to smithereens."

"On purpose?" Kate's voice came out in a squeak.

Matt's answer was deliberately sardonic. "No, it was an accident." He sighed. "They probably slipped on the bottle of fingerprint ink they found on my desk. It rolled off and smashed on the floor, spilling all over everything. They tried to clean it up with their little feet. Now I have a black and brown wood floor with matching walls."

Now Kate was shocked. "Matt, I'm scared."

He gave her a look and a small nod. "So am I," he said. "If anyone finds out about this, we'll have a full-scale panic on our hands. At the moment we are cut off from the mainland."

"They're bound to send someone to investigate eventually," Kate said.

"Not really. It's not unusual for us islanders to cut ourselves off from civilization. After all, isn't that why you came here?"

Kate nodded reluctantly. "Supplies are due in this Wednesday. I guess we'll just have to wait until then."

"Maybe not. Perhaps you'd like to take a boat to the mainland tomorrow and tell them what's happening here?"

Kate eyed him darkly. "Me, steer a boat across the ocean? In this freezing weather?" She stopped at what she was saying and laughed. "Once is enough for me," she admitted. "Besides, I'm not as desperate this time."

"Neither am I," Matt agreed. "To tell you the truth, I kind of like the excitement."

"Having aliens land in your backyard is more than just exciting."

Matt looked at her. "I was talking about us," he said softly.

Kate let that remark linger, not just because it warmed her to the core, but because it was the first time he had said anything like that to her. Now she knew for sure that something was going to happen. Maybe not tonight— But no, maybe it would be tonight! Why not? Her heart began to beat in anticipation and a sparkle stole into her eyes.

Matt broke the silence pleasantly. "Come on, let's eat."

He carried the lantern with him into the tiny cell and placed it on the floor. Kate carried in a chair, pulled it up to the round wooden table, and sat down. The candlelight flickered across Matt's face as he sat down next to her and gave her a smile that was strangely intimate.

He touched the steak in front of him and licked his finger. "Still warm," he pronounced happily. Then he examined the bottle of red wine. "Excellent year for this Burgundy—although not my number-one choice."

"Now you're a wine expert?" she teased as she produced a corkscrew from her purse.

Matt picked up a candle and held it up to a shelf above his head. To Kate's astonishment, there were a dozen or so bottles of wine stored in an overhead rack.

"St. Emilion '68s," he explained. "I bought them at an auction over twenty years ago."

Kate gazed from the wine to Matt with growing amazement. "They must be worth a fortune today."

Matt smiled, reached up, and took a bottle off the rack. He examined the label and held it up for Kate to see. She nodded. "Okay, okay, I'm impressed," she said. "But what's the occasion?"

"We are," Matt said, inserting the corkscrew and twisting it deftly. He pulled out the cork with a little pop. "We are celebrating our first date."

Kate felt suddenly embarrassed. She had preferred ambiguity to an out-and-out declaration. "Is this our first date?"

"Come to think of it, you're right. It's our second," he corrected. "Last night was our first." He laughed. "Hunting for aliens is not exactly dinner and a movie, but what the heck . . ." Kate watched as he carefully poured them each a glass of wine. "Now let's see if this stuff is as good as they said it would be."

He held his glass aloft and said grandly, "To the greatest adventure we've ever known on this island."

"It's not over yet," Kate reminded him. "But it sure beats the time that motorcycle gang roared off the ferry three years ago."

Matt shook his head. "When I said adventure, I wasn't talking about the aliens." He gave her a new and very interesting look, one that she had never seen before. "I'm still talking about us."

"Oh." She almost blushed. "Look, Matt . . ."

"Yes?"

"I-I'm not as adventurous as you seem to believe. And I can't give you any guarantees. I'm glad that we've become friends, but . . ." She put down her wineglass.

"Don't worry about it," Matt said, putting his glass down, too. "Let's just take it as it comes."

"I'm not so sure I want to take anything," Kate said. She wasn't sure what was prompting her sudden reluctance, unless it was his sudden openness. Thinking about him—being attracted to him—was one thing. Having him verbally acknowledge the rapport between them was another. Matt was such a serious, solid person that an acknowledgment seemed almost like a commitment.

But Matt didn't seem to mind. "Right now I'd just like to concentrate on what's happening at this moment."

"What about what's going on around this island right now?"

"It will come and go just like that motorcycle gang. But you and I will still be here."

But that wasn't true, and she shook her head adamantly. "You might be, but I won't. I'm leaving, remember?" She saw him grimace a little. "That's what I'm trying to tell you."

"And I'm trying to tell you that something is happening here, and you can't ignore it."

"I'm not ignoring it."

He smiled and picked up his glass. "Well, then?"

"Don't make more of it than it is, that's all."

"I don't know what it is," he said reasonably. "That's what we're going to find out." He studied her, fingering his napkin. "What's really bothering you, Kate? You're overreacting."

"No, I'm not. You are."

He lifted an eyebrow. "How's that?"

"You're a little upset about the prospect of becoming a grandfather, and you think that an instant romance is the way to cure it."

"Now *that* is ridiculous." He looked as if he truly meant it, and Kate cringed. She picked up her knife and cut into her steak, determined to bring the conversation back to herself. "Well, anyway, I can't hide out on this island for the rest of my life."

His impatience increased. "Who said that this island is a hideout? You've got to stop using it as one. You spend three years here and all you have to show for it is a FOR SALE sign in a window?" He pointed his fork at her. "That bar of yours is like a wall. You've been using it to keep all of us on one side and you on the other. Last night you finally came around to the other side, and look what happened."

She picked up her glass, a little shaken. He was right—but so was she. "Look who's talking about hiding out. What do you call this?" she asked, gesturing around her. "You live in a jail cell! Talk about walls—yours are made of iron bars."

"Temporary quarters," he said with a shrug. "My own house is too big for just me. It's a five-bedroom Victorian with three baths, two studies, a huge dining room, and a kitchen the size of a gymnasium."

"Old Man Farquil manages well in his place," she pointed out, sipping the wine. "Hey, this wine is great." It was a clumsy way to appreciate a bottle of St. Emilion whatever-it-was, but she was preoccupied.

"Glad you like it," he said gruffly, the toast forgotten. "And I'm not an old man. I'd appreciate your leaving the old-man stuff out altogether. I'm in the prime of life."

"I know you are. But you are very sensitive about it. That's what this whole conversation is about."

"No, it is not." He picked up his wineglass with an aggravated air and took a sip. "It's about— Say, you're right. This is an excellent wine." They looked at each other oddly, and then they both laughed.

"Okay, okay," she said. "Let's start over."

"All I'm asking you to do is not discount anything. Stick around for a while longer and try out the product."

"The product?" She frowned. "You mean the island?"

"I mean me. I'm the product."

"Do you come with a guarantee?"

He laughed. "If not completely satisfied, return for a full refund."

"I just might take you up on that."

He lifted his wineglass into the air. "To whatever comes."

Kate clinked her glass against his. "Whatever."

"Don't be so blasé," he said coolly. "I just might sweep you off your feet. Besides," he added, "I'm not blind, you know."

"Blind to what?"

"That dress. Your hair. Everything." His eyes swept over her, clearly indicating that he liked what he saw.

Kate looked down. It was true. She had dressed to attract him, and it was much too late to pretend that she didn't want to.

"Let your defenses down, Kate," he said softly. "I won't bite. I promise."

She looked up and caught the look in his eyes. It was smoldering. Before she could catch her breath, he leaned over and kissed her. Gently at first, tentatively bridging the gap between them, and then with a sense of command that thrilled her. His right hand moved to her back, drawing her close, and his left hand slipped around her shoulder. The kiss lasted for a deliciously long time.

When it ended, Kate sat with her eyes still closed, unwilling for it to be over. She had responded to him as naturally and as easily as if she had known him for a very long time—which indeed she had, she realized with a start. She opened her eyes and looked at him. He was no longer just the sheriff, no longer a familiar island face. He was now her lover.

He was still leaning over her, his eyes still blazing. "I've wanted to do that for a very long time," he whispered.

Kate was thrilled all over again. "Really?" She couldn't resist adding, "How long?"

"How long have you been here?"

She smiled a little. "A long time. Too long." This was followed by a rueful sigh. "As long as it's been since someone kissed me."

"Well, cheer up," he said, running a finger along the back of her neck. "It's been longer than that for me."

They gazed at each other for an intense moment, both searching and confirming what they saw, when suddenly the door flew open, and a gust of wind blew the candle out. Matt was instantly alert.

"I thought you closed that door," he said, looking up. He stood and went over to the door, shutting it firmly.

"I thought I did, too." He sat back down and they looked at each other. Then Kate smiled. "Where were we?"

Matt drew her into his arms and kissed her again, this time with a mastery that left her breathless. Her desire rose quickly, almost too quickly, she thought. It had been a long time, but Matt was so commanding and so reassuring at the same time that her defenses simply fell apart. She clung to him intently, letting the soft swirl of feelings envelop them.

Suddenly Matt pulled away. "Did you hear anything?"

"No," she said after a moment.

She thought she saw a flash of a shadow dart across the room from the corner of her eye, and she flinched. "What was that?"

Matt dropped a row of kisses down her neck that left her dizzy. "Are you trying to stop me from sweeping you off your feet?"

"No, no, I . . ." The rest of whatever she was going to say was lost as he concentrated on arousing her, of which he was doing a highly effective job. Kate leaned back and sighed deliciously, opening her eyes for a moment and then closing them again. But again something flashed by during that brief second, and her eyes flew open. Her eyes darted to a corner of his office as if she were looking for something.

"What is it, Kate?" Matt whispered in a voice that sent a wild gleam of response coursing through her. "Relax now, love." His hands traveled intimately down the sides of her body, coming to rest on her hips. "I'm going to make love to you, Kate. You know that, don't you?"

She nodded breathlessly, unable to speak.

"And we're going to do this very slowly, because we have all the time in the world. No one is here to interfere, and we're going to enjoy every lovely minute of it." Kate began to tremble. She reached up for him and they kissed again, so engrossed in each other that they didn't even notice that the cell door was starting to close.

A second later it clanged shut, and the bolt was thrown. Matt and Kate both jumped up just in time to see a shadowy figure dart out the front door. The heavy door banged shut, leaving two people imprisoned for the night.

"Well, that was a lovely meal," Matt said an hour later. "Thank you for bringing it."

"You're welcome," Kate answered, downing the rest of the wine. "It's the first time I've ever had dinner in a jail cell, and I trust it will be the last."

They had resigned themselves to their fate after banging fruitlessly on the bars for several minutes, realizing that no one was going to hear them, and that they were trapped together for the night. Fortunately they had a lovely meal laid out in front of them, and the rest of the evening seemed so delightfully inevitable that they had decided to enjoy it step by step.

Kate looked doubtfully at the twin beds chained to the wall, and Matt reassured her. "Don't worry. Dan will be by in the morning to let us out. These are actually quite comfortable. You know, I have a funny feeling that things are taking a bizarre turn in this town tonight. We'll need all the rest we can to cope with it tomorrow."

"Here we are again," Kate said, looking around.

"Trapped together for the second night by those . . . creatures."

"Maybe they're matchmakers from another planet, sent to earth to ensure that you and I remain together forever," Matt said dreamily.

"They're succeeding," she admitted. "But I wish they'd mind their own business."

"Well, I don't," Matt said. "I'm glad they keep throwing us together like this. Hell, I should have made my move sooner."

This was an interesting piece of news. "Oh, really? Well, why didn't you?"

Matt stood up and cleared the dishes into a neat little pile. Then he pushed the table over to the front of the cell and sat down on one of the beds. Kate joined him after a moment, sitting close to him.

"Are you ready to hear the story, bartender?" he asked.

"Oh, one of those." Kate nodded sagely. "Okay, shoot. After all, we've got all night."

"That winter day when your motorboat came roaring into the harbor," he began.

"What about it?"

"I was stone drunk."

Kate nodded a little, and he let that one sit for a while. Kate had always wondered about that. Everyone in town had heard about the lady Columbus who had crossed the channel in the dead of winter. It only took one round of gossip at the tavern to take care of that. And yet the irascible sheriff, usually attuned to every island event, had never come by to investigate.

"I had been hitting the bottle for over two years," Matt continued. He stopped talking and reached up to the shelf, handing Kate the picture of the woman she had seen in his Jeep.

She studied it closely. "Your wife?"

"Annie died six years ago," he explained. "A part of me went with her, I guess. First I stopped going to social events. Then I gave up on my friends. The Thursday night poker games at Flint's tavern were my last touch with civilization. I started drinking at the bar, mostly at the corner table by myself. But too many old friends and memories interfered with that. Soon I was drinking at home, alone. Finally I left my home and set up house here at the jail."

Kate thought this over, and realized something. "And you stopped drinking when I first came to the island."

"Yes," Matt admitted, not looking at her.

Kate took his hand and squeezed it gently. "So I had an influence on you," she said.

Matt smiled. "I was impressed with you. You had guts."

"Did I? I didn't know that. I thought I was running away."

"You were. So what? At least you were doing something more than drowning your sorrows in a bottle every night."

Kate put her other hand over the one she was holding. "Are you trying to tell me, Matthew Caine, that you've had a crush on me for the last three years?"

He grinned and looked up finally, a glint of confidence in his eyes. "Haven't you had a crush on me these past three years?"

"No," Kate said smoothly. "I haven't."

That caused him to sit back sharply. "Well, neither have I."

"You're lying," she crowed with delight. "You just said I stopped you from drinking."

"I said I stopped drinking the day you arrived. How would it have looked to a newcomer if the sheriff was a lush?"

Kate smiled but said nothing.

Matt wasn't finished with his confession. "I knew about your foolish boating adventure hours before you arrived."

Kate sat straight up and looked at him. "Now you're making that up."

Matt smiled as if he had a secret he had been carrying around for a long time. "The coast guard radioed me. They said some foolhardy idiot was halfway across the channel in an outboard. I was supposed to let them know if you arrived safely." He turned sideways and gave her an incredulous look. "I swore to myself that if that fool made it I'd put down the bottle for good. I was finishing off a fifth of bourbon when you appeared on the horizon." He laughed. "And that's all there was to that."

Kate studied him curiously. "You stopped drinking on a dime, just like that?"

"Sure." He shrugged. "It was time. I knew it was time." He looked at her. "But you were the catalyst."

"I guess I should be flattered."

"I guess you should."

His arms went around her and she clung to him, impressed and moved by his revelation. The attraction she had felt building up in the last two days was not an instant one, as she had thought. It was a passion born of a long and slow climb, one that was culminating now as they opened their hearts to each other.

They fell back on the bed, letting their hands talk to

each other with intimate awareness. Matt was compact and strong, and she loved the solid feel of him as he stretched out next to her.

They kissed and kissed again, lost in a timeless whirl of sensuality. Matt rained tiny, fiery kisses over her cheeks, her neck, and her shoulders, pushing at her dress impatiently.

Kate hesitated for only a second when his fingers tugged at the zipper. She shivered when it went down, and then she sighed when Matt's warm, strong hand slipped inside and found bare skin.

"So soft," he whispered, letting his hand slide around her smooth shoulders and around to her back. His voice thrilled her as much as his actions. The dress moved down imperceptibly, until at last Matt gently pushed her bra straps down. Her breasts swelled temptingly over the top of the scanty white lace bra.

Kate looked at Matt's face, and a ripple of desire went through her when she saw his eyes. They were on fire. She arched her back slightly, letting him reach underneath to unfasten the single clasp.

In a moment her breasts were bared to him, and he stared at them for a minute in wonder. "I knew you were beautiful," he breathed, "but . . ."

Then he was kissing them softly, all around at first, savoring their round firmness, and then concentrating on their rosy peaks, drawing them into his mouth and sucking gently.

Kate moaned and closed her eyes as her desire spiraled quickly. He was utterly gentle and yet subtlely insistent, drawing her with him into a world that consisted only of the two of them.

When Matt began pushing her dress down to her hips, Kate's eyes opened reluctantly. His warm hands spanned her waist and held her for a breathless moment. But Kate wasn't ready to surrender entirely to him, not yet.

He sensed her hesitation at once, and looked up at her. "What is it, Kate?"

"I—I don't want to rush things . . ."

His hands around her bare skin gave a little squeeze. "Okay."

She felt instantly contrite. "I— It isn't that I'm not . . . I mean . . ."

He smiled. "I understand."

"But—" She struggled to sit up.

"I know. It's okay." He wrapped his arms around her and held her close. It felt delicious to be held by him like this, her bare skin nestling against his strong but fully clothed body. "There's no rush," he said quietly in her ear. "It's been a long time . . ."

"For both of us," she acknowledged, turning her head so that it rested against his shoulder. Tears stung her eyes suddenly, but she blinked them back, and he continued holding her wordlessly, without demanding anything from her.

After a long while he kissed her again. Then he sat back and handed her a blanket. "Let's go to sleep," he said with such friendly persuasion that she smiled. "In the morning someone will come and let us out of here."

Kate slid out of her dress and snuggled down under the blanket. Matt extinguished the lantern so that the cell was pitch-black. She lay quietly and listened as Matt quickly undressed and slid onto the other bunk. For a moment she regretted her decision. She found herself yearning to see him, to know what his body looked like, to touch him in places she would never dare think of touching until now . . .

Silence enveloped them and then Matt said softly, "Good night, Kate."

She fell pleasantly asleep, adrift in her own yearnings.

CHAPTER
Eight

KATE AND MATT were awakened the next morning by the sound of Dick Battering's voice amplified through a loudspeaker.

"Attention, extraterrestrials. We are your friends. We will not harm you. We will take you to our leader."

Matt groaned and pulled the blanket over his head. "Our leader?" He looked at Kate, who was grinning. "I hope he doesn't mean me."

Kate leaned over and looked at Matt on the opposite bunk. "At the moment, my dear, you're the most likely candidate. It looks like we're about to be rescued." She reached for her dress and slid it on under the blanket.

"Well, I just hope I don't have to speak to any aliens until after breakfast. I am not a nice person at this hour of the morning."

He got up and climbed quickly into his clothes. Forgetting that the cell door was locked, he then banged his head trying to open it. Outside, the loudspeaker continued to blare.

"We welcome peaceful aliens."

Matt went over to the window, thrust his hands through the bars, and managed to open the shutter halfway. A cool chill swept through the cell, along with Dick Battering's amplified voice.

"We will not harm you. Where are you hiding?"

Matt let out a long singing call to him. "Yooohoooo ... Earthling..." He turned and looked at Kate, who was laughing behind her hands. "Yooohoooo ... over here. Help us! We're locked in the jail."

And through the winter morning air, the high school principal's voice shook with fear. "Oh, my God." His voice reverberated around the street. "Hey, George, Hal, Dan ... hey, guys. I found them. The E.T.s They're at the jail."

Matt wasn't finished. "Yoooohoooo ... Earthling!"

"Yes ... uh—what is it?"

"Food," Matt said loudly, in a high squeak. "We are hungry. We haven't eaten in over ten thousand light years. Bring us food. We will not harm you."

"And we won't harm you either," Dick promised earnestly.

Kate could hear the principal running down the street, hollering for everyone else. She got up in time to see them congregating near Digger's store. George Digger came out with an armload of groceries and then they were met by a half dozen others including Roy Wilmot, Stan Farquil, Jack Gardner, and Grady Mason, who had a fishing net draped across his shoulder.

"This is precious," Kate said. "They look so serious."

Matt was laughing. His laughter was contagious and

a few seconds later Kate was chortling as well.

"Shhh, shhh." She waved him to be quiet. "Here they come."

Slowly the contingency made its way up Main Street toward the jail cell. Jack Gardner was in the lead, carrying a large crowbar.

Kate couldn't resist saying something. She tried her best to change her voice. "Throw down your weapons," she said in a shrill whine.

The group halted in their tracks and backed off a little. "Throw down your weapons," Kate repeated. "We have blasters aimed at you. If you do not obey, we will disintegrate your clothes off your bodies."

The crowbar fell from Jack Gardner's hand. The look on his face was so shocked that Matt nearly fell on the floor from laughter.

"Shhh," Kate warned, tapping him sternly.

Matt got up and tried another ploy. "Take off your hats. We do not trust people who wear hats."

The hats practically flew off everyone's head. By now Matt and Kate were in hysterics.

George Digger lifted up the grocery bags. "We have food for you."

"Yeah, food," Dan Shere added eagerly. "If you want, I can cook something . . . I mean if you like food cooked? You do like food cooked, don't you?"

"Cooked?" Kate managed to choke between peals of laughter. "What is cooked?"

Jack Gardner turned to Dan and scolded him. "You idiot. You're talking to aliens. They might not eat the way we do."

"Maybe they don't have mouths like us," George added in a loud whisper.

Matt was ready with another line. "Foolish earthlings. Of course we have mouths. One for eating and another one for talking."

That did it. Kate burst into uproarious laughter and Matt followed. By the time the E.T. hunters realized they had been had, Matt and Kate were holding onto each other and howling.

George Digger was the first to enter the jail. The others followed in a solemn little line. "Not funny, Matt," George scolded him. "You're not funny at all."

But Jack Gardner was laughing. "Now that's the Sheriff Caine I used to know." He gave Matt a hearty pat on the back through the bars, congratulating him for pulling it off so well. "You're still the best practical joker on the island."

George Digger still wasn't laughing. "Inappropriate," he said, shaking his head. "This is serious business."

Matt tried to wipe the smile from his face. "Sorry, George. We couldn't resist. You guys looked so serious out there."

While Dan opened the cell door, the others began to look around the disheveled office. Once they spotted the footprints, the rest was easy to deduce.

"They deliberately came here to destroy the radio," Jack Gardner announced with growing alarm. He bent down and touched the footprints. "There were three, maybe four of the creatures in here."

They all crowded around Matt and fired questions at him.

"Did they attack you, Sheriff?"

"No."

"Do they have ray guns?"

"No."

"Are they heterosexual?"

Matt froze at that one, and looked at Grady Mason, who was actually waiting for an answer.

Kate stepped forward and examined the food in George's grocery bag. While the men gathered around Matt asking questions, she found a skillet and quietly began making breakfast. By the time Matt finished organizing them into three separate posses, Kate had managed to scramble some eggs and had set the table in the cell.

Matt gave final instructions. "George and Jack, go north to the Jaspar farm and see what you find. Al and Roy, take Glendale Road all the way to the end. Hal Freedy and Dan, go south. We'll reconnoiter at Kate's tavern around noon. Meanwhile see if you can find someone willing to drive a boat to the mainland. I want the authorities out here by sundown."

"I'll go." It was Hal Freedy. He pushed his way forward. "I can get my speedboat into the water by noon and be across the channel in less than two hours. I won't come back without the entire U.S. Army, even if I have to speak to the President himself."

He ran out so fast that Matt could only call to him from the door. "Don't over do it, Hal. Do you hear me? It's not as bad as all that."

After everyone had gone, Kate took Matt by the arm and led him gently into the cell. "Now calm down," she said soothingly. "You certainly have them all busy this morning."

Matt relaxed when he saw the breakfast table. "Hey, this is great. Thanks." He gave her an impish grin. "I managed to get rid of that troublemaker Freedy. That should give me enough time to finish repairing the radio."

Kate poured his coffee. "What are you going to tell the authorities?"

Matt was stumped. "I haven't thought about that yet. If I tell them the truth, they'll think I'm nuts. On the other hand, we saw what we saw, right?"

Kate shook her head. "It seems to me you could be just a little bit frightened by them. I know I am."

Matt shook his head. "So far they've been more mischievous than dangerous, wouldn't you agree?"

"I suppose you're right. But do you think they're really from another planet?" It was the first time she had asked him point-blank about that aspect of it.

Matt shrugged. "I'm only sure of one thing." He put down his fork and looked at her. "You and I have something going here."

"Please, Matt. I was talking about aliens. Why don't you ever want to talk about that?"

Matt began eating again. "Maybe they heard that your tavern was for sale and they've come to make you an offer you can't refuse."

"If they want it, they can have it—cheap."

Matt stopped eating and looked at her in hurt surprise. "You want out that badly?"

Kate nodded. "Don't look at me that way. I told you it's time for me to get on with my life."

"And you have. Right here, now. What do you call what we're doing together?"

"Eating breakfast." She gave him a hard look. "At least we're trying to eat. If you wouldn't keep putting a damper on things."

"All I'm saying is—"

Kate touched his hand and silenced him. "I know what you're saying. Let's eat, okay?"

* * *

By late afternoon, the outside of Kate's tavern looked more like the entrance to a hit drive-in movie than a parking lot. The cars were wedged in five-rows deep and in some places they actually blocked Main Street altogether. People were still driving up and deserting their cars and Jeeps along the sidewalks and alleys, and walking the distance to the tavern.

Inside, there was no room to sit, and little room to stand or breathe. Three times Kate had to empty the overflowing cash from her register. She had bought out half of George Digger's store, and still she had run out of hamburger buns and bread. Flint kept revising the menu, continually crossing things out as the food supply steadily dwindled. Finally at four o'clock, the menu was thrown out. They had run out of food.

The liquor supply hadn't fared any better. Winter was the slow season, but because of the crisis, her entire two-month supply of booze was now down to a bottle of bourbon, two bottles of scotch, a pint of tequila, and three bottles of champagne, which had come from an untouched case of twelve bottles only four hours ago.

Luckily there was enough beer on tap to last at least two more days, but with the phones dead, she had no way of ordering more.

She threw up her arms in happy defeat. "After this, I'm going on a long-needed vacation."

Flint was cleaning out the register for the fourth time that afternoon. He plunked the money into her lap and laughed. "If I didn't know you better, I'd swear this whole UFO incident was your idea to boost business."

Kate looked up at the ceiling. "Thank you, E.T.—now phone home, and leave—please!"

But Flint wasn't finished. "It also brought you and Matt something unexpected, didn't it?"

Kate whipped around and looked at him. It was the most personal thing he had said to her in three years.

"Hey, Kate! Let's have five more beers!" It was George Digger's voice. He and his cohorts had finished their search of the island as Matt had instructed and were now working on their third round of beers. So was everyone else in the tavern.

This was the place to be, and everyone was there to hear what the sheriff had to say. The only problem was that Matt was four hours late. If he didn't show up soon, Kate figured, he'd be responsible for the inebriated condition of the entire population of Blackwell's Island.

"Hey, Kate! What's holding up the drinks?"

"Yeah—and where's our burgers?"

"Where's our sandwiches?"

"Where's the sheriff?"

That last question got everyone agreeing. "Someone ought to go over to the jail and get him."

"Maybe he locked himself in again."

"Or the E.T.'s kidnapped him?" That produced a round of laughter.

Flint looked at Kate and then gazed around the tavern. "I've never seen them all like this. I'd say most of the population of this island is now safely anesthetized."

"Anesthetized, yes—safely, no." Matt's voice came from the doorway to the kitchen. Kate turned around to see him beckoning furtively from the open door. "Come in here, fast."

Before anyone spotted them, Kate backed out of the bar and scooted into the kitchen. The next thing she knew, she was swept into Matt's arms. He gave her a long, slow kiss that melted away her frustration and fatigue. Then, before she could catch her breath, he handed her a present wrapped in blue foil with a red ribbon around it. There was a card attached.

Kate was so glad to see him that she didn't care about aliens, she didn't care about business, and she didn't care what anyone thought. She only wanted to be right where she was—in Matt's arms. "Where have you been all afternoon?" she asked.

"Making your present," he answered slyly.

Kate looked at the gift. "What about the radio?"

"What about it?"

She looked at him as if he were crazy. "Well, is it fixed?"

Matt shrugged. "It's unfixable. We'll just have to wait for Freedy to get us help from the mainland. Meanwhile, I spent the afternoon making you a gift. It's for the bar."

Kate was growing a little perturbed. "For the bar? I don't need anything for the bar. I'm selling it, remember?"

"No, you are not." It was nothing less than an order, but he said it with such obvious happiness, that she simply looked at him in complete bafflement.

"Oh, Matt. Did you know this place is one step away from a full-scale riot. Why didn't you come sooner?"

He pointed at the present and smiled.

"That's no excuse." But she couldn't help smiling back. "Who would have believed that I would actually look forward to one of your official visits to handle a riot?"

But Matt wasn't interested in official business. "How about going for a drive with me tonight? I've got to patrol the island all night to make sure those folks out there don't do anything too crazy until the authorities get here. I can use the company and, besides, we have a lot to talk about."

"We do?" Kate couldn't believe it. Matt was moving things between them a lot faster than she wanted to go. She had been planning to leave, to start a new life—and here was this man cheerfully making plans for her to stay. True, she had been wildly attracted to him and, true, he was the first man she had become involved with in a long time, but that didn't mean she was going to be distracted from her goals. No way. He was being presumptuous, and she sought a gentle way to give him the message loud and clear.

"Look, Matt . . . I think you've got the wrong idea about us."

"No, I don't."

"Yes, I'm afraid you do. You see, I'm leaving the island, hopefully by winter's end—and I'm not coming back."

"You're not leaving." He said it flatly, as if there could be no doubt, and her temper began to flare.

She tried again. "Yes, I am. I'm selling this place, remember?"

Suddenly he marched out of the kitchen and into the crowded tavern.

"Hey, look, it's the sheriff."

"Hey, Matt!"

"Matt?"

"Sheriff, what's happening with the radio?"

"Where are the aliens?"

"Are they dangerous?"

"Matt?"

"Matt?"

"Hey . . . *Sheriff*!"

Matt totally ignored the pressing crowd, as if the

only crisis at the moment was a personal one between the two of them. As she stood watching from the kitchen, Matt resolutely pushed and shoved his way across to the entrance. Sticking his hand into the front window, he removed her FOR SALE sign.

In no time at all, Kate was pushing and shoving her way to the front of the tavern as well. When she reached him, the confrontation began. She pointed at the sign in his hand.

"Put it back!"

"No."

"Put it back. I'm selling and that's final."

Matt didn't take his eyes from hers. "You're not selling anything. You're not running away again."

"That's my business!"

He shook his head and looked at everyone in the tavern. They were looking back at him, awaiting word on the crisis.

"That's my business," Kate repeated.

"No, that's our business." Matt looked around the room, the glint of an idea forming in his eyes. "Isn't that right, folks? Isn't that our business? We don't want Kate to leave, do we?"

Everyone voiced an instant opinion. "No!" they all yelled.

Matt looked triumphantly at Kate. "You see, we all love you."

Kate yelled back, "I think you're all crazy!" She was shooting sparks at him with her eyes, and she didn't intend to say more—not in front of all these people. Matt assessed the crowd again and then looked back at Kate. He was fingering the FOR SALE sign thoughtfully.

"What's going on, Matt?" Dan Shere asked, effectively breaking the tension. "Did you find out anything?"

Matt straightened, and widened his stance. Kate noticed how effortlessly he could change into his sheriff's demeanor. "Now listen up," he announced, his usual authority taking over. "Help is on the way. Hal Freedy drove his boat to the coast to get help. By tomorrow morning, the coast guard, or the army, or the National Guard, or *someone* will be here to find these little creatures. Meanwhile, we do nothing."

"What do you mean, nothing?" George Digger called out in disgust.

The rest of the crowd agreed and Matt had to quiet them down. "I mean that you all sober up with some strong coffee, and drive home safely. Stay home tonight, and don't go looking for any E.T.s."

A hum of disapproval went through the place.

Matt gave them a second warning. "Do I make myself clear?" He looked at George Digger and Jack Gardner when he said it.

They both nodded glumly, and so did everyone else.

Kate was standing next to him. She put out her hand, palm up. "Very good, Sheriff. May I have my sign back now?"

He didn't give it to her. Instead, he glared at her, marched out the door and down the street, and headed back to the jail.

Kate yelled to the back of the bar where Flint was leaning against the wall, "Toss me my coat."

Flint obeyed, and a second later it came sailing over everyone's heads and landed in her arms. She was out the door with one arm in her coat, fighting against the bitter wind as she raced after him. The sun had almost set, but the reddish tinge still left in the sky lit her way.

She finally caught up with him three blocks away in front of his office.

"Matthew Caine," she called out angrily. "You'd better stop right now."

But he kept walking briskly without paying her the slightest attention.

"I'm warning you!" And with that she scooped up a handful of snow and shaped it quickly into a large snowball. After packing it good and tight, she aimed it right at his head. She was only a little off; it got him on the lower back.

And it did make him stop.

Kate reloaded with another handful, getting closer this time for another try at a head shot. She let it go briskly, but Matt was too quick. Using her FOR SALE sign as a bat, he knocked her second shot away with ease.

"Not a bad pitch, but I used to play for the Blackwell Bombers!" he called out cheerfully. "Now you'll find out why they called me the Home Run King."

This only fired Kate's competitive spirit as well as her anger. She moved slealthily closer and fired two more rounds at him. He knocked both away with ease. Again she reloaded, one in each hand, while he stood there grinning and swinging the sign from one hand to the other. But while he was showing off, twirling the sign in the air and catching it on its way down, she placed a third snowball in her pocket.

Matt batted the first one away, and then the next, taunting her to try again. "I told you I was a good batter," he said. "You can't hit me, Kate, so give it up."

She stood with her hands empty, and watched as he tucked the sign under his arm, as if to indicate that it was staying where it was. His look was so boyishly triumphant that she couldn't resist smiling.

She threw her arms up with an air of defeat. "You win, lover boy." He smiled back as she ran over to him and put her hands on his shoulders. They were both still smiling fiercely, but Matt obviously didn't trust her. He held the sign firmly in his left hand, keeping it behind him as he drew her close with the other arm. She didn't resist.

"Now I'm going to kiss you," he announced. "And we are going to stop all this foolishness."

She was gazing into his eyes. "All right," she said sweetly, reaching into her pocket for the snowball.

His lips came toward hers, but they never touched. In the next instant he let out a yelp. Kate had rammed the snowball down his back, and it lodged somewhere inside his shirt, above his belt. He dropped the sign and began tugging at his shirt to remove the snowball, but Kate wasn't finished.

Before he could remove it, Kate picked up the sign and whacked him firmly on the back, making definite contact with the snowball. She could feel it flattening against his back.

It flaked out from behind him in pieces as he squinted at her in surprise. His face had changed drastically. "So, you want to play, huh?"

He picked up a handful of snow and, before she could protect herself, he let her have it full in the chest.

But the snow easily dropped off and, turning on her heel, she headed back to her bar, triumphantly holding her sign. She should have continued to look behind her.

"Gotcha!" Matt's arms wrapped around her waist and an instant later she found herself being dragged along the street toward a huge snowdrift. But in the ensuing struggle, Matt lost his balance and the two of them went barreling down together, completely buried up to their necks in fluffy white powder.

He was laughing.

She wasn't.

"I fail to see the humor in all this."

"Aw, come on, Kate. Lighten up. It's going to be a long night. How about joining me for dinner again?"

"I'm not interested."

"Maybe a late-night snack."

"No."

Matt wouldn't give up. "How about you and I open up another bottle of that St. Emilion?"

That one almost stopped her. That wine had been a rare treat.

He saw her hesitate and pressed his attack. "Nineteen-thirty was a good year for wine," he said.

But Kate held her ground. She shook her head. "No, thanks. You'll only start up on me again."

"What if I promise not to say anything about your leaving?"

"You will."

"I won't. I promise. If I do, you can leave."

She thought it over. "If you do, I'm going to dump more snow on that thick head of yours."

"You can pour wine on it for all I care." He gave her a devastatingly charming smile and stretched out his hand. "Madame, if you'd be so kind as to join me inside?"

Kate shook her head. "Let's go to my place. Yours is . . . unsafe."

"Are you afraid the aliens will come back and attack us?" His tone was playful.

"I'm afraid of you."

He lifted an eyebrow. "Glad to see I'm having an

effect on you." He stood up. "Let's get the wine." She stood up and joined him. Together they walked down the now-darkened street.

"It's going to be quite crowded at your place," he said as they crunched through the snow. "There won't be any privacy."

"I know. I don't want you getting any ideas."

He stopped in the middle of the street and took her by the shoulders. "Now, look here, Kate. Let's get one thing straight. If I want to make love to you, I will. Even if it's in the back room of the bar. You can't tell me you don't want to. I said I wouldn't rush you, and I haven't. But you're hiding your head in the sand." She opened her mouth to answer him, but he wouldn't let her talk. "And another thing. You can't keep running away. First from what's-his-name, and now from me." She looked at him obstinately. "Don't tell me you can respond to me the way you did last night, and then just walk away from it."

Kate explained hesitantly. "I just don't want to lead you on. There's no future in us."

Matt smiled, but the gleam in his eye told her that he wasn't at all convinced. "I just wanted to be alone with you tonight. The future—that's another thing. We are alone at the moment, and that's all I'm thinking about right now."

They walked back to her place in silence. The crunching snow was the only sound in the still evening, and the air had that quiet, expectant quality, as if it would snow again at any time. Kate felt strangely dissatisfied about the stance she had taken with him. She wondered if by chance she was making a fool of herself. He had made her a present, and she hadn't even looked at it. For the first time, she wondered what it was.

As they neared the bar, she could see all the candles flickering in the windows—but something was missing.

"The cars," she exclaimed, "they're all gone."

They quickened their pace and went inside. The place was empty. Flint sat alone at the bar, the wrapped present Matt had brought sitting unopened next to him. Kate ran over and picked it up.

"You've got troubles now," Flint informed them gloomily.

The old man poured himself a shot from the last of the bourbon and drank it down before continuing. He was obviously very upset, and Kate and Matt exchanged worried glances. Flint never got upset about anything. Finally he told them what had happened. "They found Hal Freedy's boat."

Kate's stomach dropped. "What do you mean—they found it?"

Matt sat down heavily on a stool and ran his hands through his hair. "Tell me everything."

"It floated up onto South Beach about a half hour ago. There was a huge, gaping hole in the bow."

Matt's face froze. "What about Hal?"

"There was no sign of him."

Kate closed her eyes and tried to blink back tears, but it was no use. Fear rose up right behind the grief, and she clutched onto the bar for support. "He must have hit something in the water," she said, her voice faltering.

Flint gave her a look that clearly expressed his doubt, but he repeated what she said. "Yeah, you're right. He must have hit something."

Kate grabbed Matt's arm. She was shaking.

Matt was frowning and thinking hard. "Perhaps he didn't hit anything at all," he suggested.

Kate looked at him quizzically.

"Perhaps—" He tried to continue, but lost his voice for a second. When he regained his composure, he looked at Kate and took a deep breath. "Perhaps something hit him."

CHAPTER
Nine

CAR LIGHTS FLOODED the snowy beach, casting an eerie projection on Hal Freedy's speedboat. As hundreds of residents gathered nervously around, Matt knelt down to examine the splintered gash in the bow.

Kate stood over him. In her hand was the gift he had given her, still unopened. She placed it on the bow of the speedboat and surveyed the damage. "It may have been foggy out there," she suggested. "Maybe he hit a log or something?"

Matt shook his head. "This boat was standing still when something brushed alongside it. Look at these splinters."

Kate obeyed, and so did the surrounding crowd. Matt beamed his flashlight on the gash. "If he had rammed something, this fiberglass hull would have a hole in it the size of a basketball." He rubbed his fingers along the slash and examined what was on them. "It's orange paint," he stated. He looked at Kate and thought hard. "An orange boat rubbed against this hull."

"Or an orange something," George Digger added nervously. He had a shotgun slung over one shoulder, which he opened conspicuously to check the bullets.

Matt gestured at the gun. "You planning on using that thing tonight, George?"

George looked around for support from the community and got it. "Yes, I am planning that," he answered. "If something gives me a good reason to, that is."

Kate looked around at everyone. The mood was definitely paranoid. "This is crazy," she said. "Hal probably got hit by something in the fog and fell overboard."

"That's a pretty pessimistic attitude, Kate," Matt said as he got up and addressed the crowd. "For all we know, Freedy got a lift to the mainland by the very boat that hit him. At this moment he's probably sitting in the harbor coast guard station trying to convince a bunch of bored servicemen that we've been invaded by creatures from another planet."

Kate remembered something and beamed. "The orange paint," she stated. "Aren't the coast guard colors orange and blue?"

Matt gave her an approving smile. "I believe you're right."

But George Digger wasn't convinced. "They'd have sent a helicopter by now."

"In this fog?" Matt laughed. "Don't be ridiculous. You're getting yourself all worked up over nothing."

Jack Gardner pointed at the hull. "You call that nothing? I say we split up into three separate groups and go looking for these creatures before they come looking for us."

The crowd mumbled in agreement.

But Matt wasn't ready to let them do that. Kate looked at him, wondering if he could handle the riot that was brewing. One look at his uncompromising profile reminded her that he could. When Matt decided to take charge of something, there was no stopping him. She watched as he stood on top of Freedy's boat and spoke to the townspeople.

"Now listen good, everyone, because I'm not going to repeat myself. You will disperse and go home. I'll have no groups of self-proclaimed rampaging soldiers running around this island with loaded weapons. Someone could get seriously hurt or even killed. I've seen this type of hysteria before, and I can tell you it is dangerous."

George Digger stepped forward with a counter argument. "We've been patient long enough, Matt. Those creatures locked you in a jail cell, don't you remember? *They're* the dangerous ones, and we're going after them tonight."

The crowd murmured darkly in agreement. Jack Gardner was already marching to his truck with Dan Shere following behind. Matt called out to his deputy.

"Just where the hell do you think you're going, Dan?"

Dan looked at Matt. Then he shrugged and stood there indecisively.

Jack Gardner did the talking for him. He raised his shotgun and yelled back, "We're going after those monsters."

At those words everyone started to head for their cars. It would have been mayhem if Matt hadn't stopped them. He grabbed George Digger's gun, pointed it in the air, and pulled the trigger.

The blast sent a ringing sound through Kate's ears.

Everyone stopped where he was and turned to Matt. He waited for their undivided attention.

"I am the law on this island."

There was a lot of disgruntled mumbling, but no one moved. Kate looked at Matt in awe. He had always been commanding, but this was a side of him she had not seen before. He was tough, aggressive and almost scary. No one there was going to challenge him, that much was clear. He waited a few more seconds, surveying the group to make sure they were listening."

"It's going down to twenty degrees tonight. Most of you have fireplaces in your homes and plenty of wood. I suggest you stay at home and feed those fires until we can get electricity restored on this island. Otherwise, aliens will be the least of your problems."

Someone called out, "What if they attack someone?"

Matt answered swiftly, "Has anyone been attacked?"

There was no answer at first. Florence Wilmot started forward, thought twice, and backed away. Kate saw Grady Mason and his wife conferring on the side. A group of men were reloading their shotguns, and Dick Battering was talking privately with a dozen or so high school students wearing purple and green Blackwell High jackets.

One of the teenagers came forward and raised his hand. "Sheriff, it's me, Gary Sanders. Can I ask you something?"

Matt squinted in the headlights as the boy made his way through the crowd and over to where Matt stood on the boat.

"I'd like to make a suggestion if I may?"

Matt shook his head. "I'd rather you didn't, son. This is a very nervous group of people and I've got a feeling that any suggestions other than my own could be detrimental."

Kate sensed the mood changing in the crowd. It went from grudging respect to anger at Matt, and she thought that perhaps he was going too far. She stepped up behind him and tapped him gently on the shoulder.

Matt looked down at her and the crowd waited.

"I think you should let him speak," she suggested.

"Oh, you do, do you?" Matt answered wearily.

Kate nodded her head. "I know this young man and I know his parents."

Gary's parents were standing near the far side of the speedboat and they waved encouragingly at Matt. He acknowledged them gruffly and nodded a hello before looking back at Kate.

Kate pressed her advantage. "You've been doing all the talking. They need to hear someone else back you up. Let him say what's on his mind. Maybe he can defuse the situation. He looks like a reasonable kid."

"I'm just doing my job," Matt argued in a whisper.

Kate shook her head firmly. "You can use a little help. Besides, yours isn't the only opinion that counts." She shrugged. "Who knows, maybe a teenager will be able to shame them into giving up this ridiculous mission of theirs." She nodded convincingly. "I saw it in a movie once, and it worked."

Matt let out a heavy sigh. "You saw this happen in a movie, huh?" He looked at Gary and then back at Kate. "Well, I hope you're right," he said glumly, stepping down. He gestured at the pedestal offered by the boat, giving Gary the stage.

Gary jumped up on the boat and looked around at everyone. Then he leaned down and whispered loudly into the sheriff's ear so that only Kate, George Digger, and a few others could hear him.

"I think they're already here," he said, squinting at the crowd.

Matt looked as puzzled as Kate. "What do you mean, *they* are already here? *Who* is here?"

"Them," Gary answered. "The aliens."

Matt's face fell. He looked at Kate, who looked down, already knowing she had made a mistake.

"Really, Sheriff," Gary pleaded. "They could be among us right now."

Matt tried to summon a smile at Gary's histrionics in an attempt to downplay them. "They're only about four-feet high, son. I think I'd recognize them."

"Yes, but they can disguise themselves to look just like humans. They can take on our shapes and walk around inside of them. I saw it once in a movie."

"In a movie?"

The kid nodded and Matt glanced at Kate. "He saw it in a movie." Kate cringed.

But Gary sounded so knowledgeable that people began nodding as if hypnotized, and looked furtively among themselves for signs of an intruder.

Gary wasn't finished. He addressed the crowd. "They could even look like someone's husband or brother or"—he looked at Matt and added—"even the sheriff!"

Roy and Florence Wilmot suddenly looked at each other as though they had never seen each other before. Then they began inching away from each other. Kate watched, amazed, as other people did versions of the same thing, and soon a new ripple of fear was coursing through the crowd. Matt glared at Kate and she let out a sigh.

"I think you can step down now, Gary," she said.

The boy went back to his friends and Matt watched as he conferred with the principal.

"Okay, folks, let's call it a night."

No one moved.

"I said, GO HOME—now!"

The townspeople still hesitated and Kate was positive that nothing Matt could say would move them.

But she was wrong.

Matt took a breath and let out a final warning. "This beach is closed for the winter. You are all trespassing. I will write out a one-hundred-dollar citation to anyone left on this beach after five more minutes." To emphasize this, Matt took out his ticket book and looked directly at George Digger.

The grocer took his gun back from Matt and quickly turned to leave the scene. Kate stifled a laugh. When all else failed, money seemed to do the trick.

It worked. Upon seeing their leader in retreat, everyone followed suit. People slowly began to disperse, but off to the side Dick Battering was still listening avidly to Gary's ideas.

Kate looked at them suspiciously. Then the principal broke away and walked over to Dan and Jack, who were preparing to leave. He conferred with them earnestly and from time to time they all looked up at Matt.

Matt jumped down from the speedboat and met Kate in the snow. "The movies, huh?"

Kate shrugged. "It worked for Henry Fonda."

"Well, I've got a long night ahead of me. I've got to patrol the island and make sure nobody does anything stupid. You wouldn't want to keep me company, would you?"

Kate did want to, but she hesitated just the same. The

situation here was highly volatile, and she sensed that Matt was using that as a way to get close to her. She had made it plain that she didn't want to rush into anything, and Matt had made it equally plain that he did. Obviously the sensible thing to do was to cool things down.

"I think I'll just . . . mosey on home," she said, trying to sound light. "It's getting late and I don't want to, uh, interfere with your work."

Matt surprised her. "Okay," was all he said, and she found herself strangely disappointed that he hadn't pursued it. He went back to his Jeep without another word.

One by one, the cars drove away from the beach. Kate sat down on the hull of the speedboat and looked out at the waves. She gave a fleeting thought to poor Hal Freedy, whom she hoped was sitting comfortably in the office of the coast guard on the mainland. Then her thoughts returned to Matt. She still hadn't opened the present he had given her. It was still resting on the boat and she picked it up to examine it.

She couldn't help being overwhelmed by unbidden feelings of affection for Matt. He had probably worked on this gift all afternoon. She shook the box slightly, wondering if maybe she shouldn't open it. Maybe she should just give it back. She had sworn that her relationship with Matt was strictly tentative, and there was no point in encouraging him. Turning into the wind, she shook her hair around her face and tried to feel independent and carefree. She had never had a casual fling with a man and she wasn't sure how one should act in such a situation.

But the box was staring her in the face and, after a while, curiosity got the better of her. She gave in and tore off the paper. The top of the box came off easily, and she adjusted her eyes to the darkness and peered inside.

After a moment she lifted out a carved wooden plaque, evidently intended to be hung outside the tavern above the entrance. In the retreating headlights of the cars she made out the words, KATE'S PLACE.

The plaque fell heavily into her lap. It was a lovely, thoughtful gift, one that had obviously required personal thought, time, and attention. She pictured him working all afternoon to finish it and felt a little guilty at the cavalier way she was treating him.

Still, he didn't know everything about her. She had needed this time to be alone and to collect herself. But as she sat by herself, bathed in the light of the last departing cars, she wondered if maybe, just maybe, she was running away again. It had only been a few days, but she felt as if she had been involved with Matt for three years. She thought about him very carefully, thought about all the times they had encountered each other. She had to admit to herself that deep down, she had admired him for a long time. Maybe the intimacy that had blossomed between them wasn't so sudden after all.

But she needed more time to think. This relationship, if that's what it was, was too capsulized. The unusual crisis enveloping the island had trapped them together, and it wasn't a fair way to judge what was happening. Maybe if they had had something of a real courtship . . .

She sat lost in thought for a long time, until at last the chill wind from the ocean reminded her that she had better get back. She picked up the plaque in her lap and put it back into the box. Then it dawned on her. She stood up and shouted toward the road, "HEY, WAIT FOR ME!"

It was no use. She ran up the beach and waved frantically at the taillights of the final car as it turned into the dark street. But it drove slowly on, oblivious to her presence, and soon it disappeared around a corner. She looked around and shivered. She was all alone on the cold beach. Plunking down in despair, she calculated the two-hour walk back into town. With any luck it wouldn't snow again for a while.

But luck was not on her side. As if her thoughts had triggered the heavens, a light snow began to fall on the beach, the soft flakes melting as they hit the ocean. With a final sigh, she got up and began the long walk into town, alone.

"Alone?" She stopped in her tracks and spoke aloud. "With those creatures out there?"

She looked around nervously to make sure she wasn't being followed, and then chided herself for her silliness. But it was hard to be sensible in the cold, wet darkness. It was late and she was tired. And for all she knew, she was being . . . watched.

She now bitterly regretted her last words to Matt, but it was too late. Putting her head down against the steady flow of wind, she ploughed on into the darkness, heading into town.

Exhausted after her two-hour walk the night before, Kate overslept by five hours. Flint managed to open the tavern, but with food supplies practically nonexistent, coffee was the only thing on the menu all afternoon.

She gazed out at the harbor from her bedroom window on the second floor. The snowstorm had finally ended, leaving behind a heavy blanket at least four-feet deep. More was predicted for this evening, according to the radio, and she thought that ought to keep everyone at home. But she was wrong.

When she finally got downstairs, she was met by a warm cup of coffee, thoughtfully prepared by Flint. No one was in the place, and she took that to mean that everyone had obeyed Matt's orders and stayed home. She walked over to the front door and peered outside. The main road in front of her place hadn't been plowed yet.

"That's strange," she said. "It's almost two o'clock. You'd think the Public Works' fellows would have the plows out by now."

Flint laughed. "The Public Works Department consists of Dan Shere and Jack Gardner driving our one plow down Main Street and then around the whole island." He walked over to the window and shook his head. "Darn snow's already starting to melt. Main Street will be a frozen sheet of ice just as soon as the temperature drops at sundown. Then we'll be in trouble."

"Where are they?" Kate asked, not really sure she wanted to know.

Flint shrugged. "I haven't seen a soul all morning. I figure Dan and Jack are sobering up someplace out by Route 22. As for Matt, he's probably in his office. I suppose he was up half the night patrolling the island. If he was, I'm sure it didn't do much good. Those idiots were like an army without a compass. I saw them crisscrossing back and forth until all hours of the night looking for aliens." Flint wasn't usually a talkative sort, but something had gotten his goat, Kate could tell. He looked at Kate as if to say something more. Then he stopped and drew back and was about to turn away and she pursued it quickly.

"What is it?"

Flint shrugged. "Uh, it's nothing."

But Kate wasn't about to let him off the hook. "No, what is it? You were about to say something."

He thought for a second. "Some kids were in here last night accusing me of being an alien in disguise." He laughed sharply and tried to talk his way out of it, but Kate suspected that was not what he had on his mind. "What an imagination those kids have," he went on, shaking his head. "And that idiot principal wanted to take blood samples from me to make sure that I was a human being." He shook his head again and tried to walk back into the kitchen, but Kate wanted to know what was really on his mind.

"You're not telling me everything. What were you really going to tell me?"

Flint had his back to her. He didn't bother to turn around, but spoke to the kitchen door instead.

"You and Matt had a tiff yesterday?"

Kate was surprised. Flint never mixed in anyone else's business. "And if we did?"

Flint still hadn't turned around. "It's none of my business, but I think you ought to reconsider selling this place. At least until you are sure of where you're going." He turned around and looked at her. He was examining her with his eyes as if he could read her mind. "Just where do you think you're going, anyway?" He answered that question himself. "You have no idea, do you?"

"I'm leaving," she said.

"More like running, to me." He leaned against the door and put his pipe in his mouth, watching her with that steady, unnerving gaze.

Kate squirmed. He had never spoken more than a

few sentences to her at a time in the three years since she had been here. She fancied she had had a pleasant, mutual understanding with him. Suddenly he was breaking that silent code as if it had never existed, as if he had been so reticent all these years simply because he had nothing to say.

She sipped her coffee with false casualness and peeked at him over the rim. He was candidly sizing her up.

"Kate, I'm going to give you two words of advice," he said, "and then I'm not going to say another thing."

If Kate had ever been nervous in her life, it was nothing compared to the overwhelming trepidation she felt now. Flint, who had never said anything to her, was now about to say something of obvious importance. After three years, it was obviously very important indeed. Her heart pounded as she sipped more coffee and nodded helplessly.

But the old man took his time. He ignored her nerves as he thought for a minute, summoning and ordering his thoughts.

Finally, signalling that he was ready, Flint put down his pipe and ambled over to her. He stood on the bartender's side of the bar opposite from where she was perched on a barstool.

"Well?" Kate asked finally when she could stand no more. "What's your advice?"

Flint looked her straight in the eyes and blurted out his answer. "Get married."

Kate gulped. She looked at him and waited for more, but there was no more. He turned away and headed back to the kitchen door with his customary unhurried gait.

She couldn't let it go at that. "That's it? That's your great advice?"

Without answering her, Flint pushed open the door and went into the kitchen, letting the door swing back and forth behind him.

CHAPTER
Ten

TRUDGING THROUGH four-foot snowbanks, Kate finally made it over to the jail. It was nearly sundown and, just as Flint had predicted, Main Street was starting to freeze over. She couldn't understand how the sheriff could be so lackadaisical as to allow the island to fall apart so easily. Even if he had been out all night, that was no excuse for sleeping the entire day away.

She knocked on his door. "Matt, it's me."

His gruff voice answered her. "It's open."

Kate kicked the snow from her boots and went inside. The office was quite cool. Matt was lying peacefully on a cot in the jail cell reading a *Field and Stream* magazine. She blinked when she saw him. He looked terrible. He was unshaven and was still wearing his clothes from the day before. By his side was an empty bottle of very good wine. He waved a lazy hello and went right on reading.

Kate went over and noted the cover story, peering through the bars. "'Surviving Mt. Washington's Worst Blizzard,'" she said aloud. "Any advice in there for us snowbound islanders?"

"Yeah," he barked. "Keep inside, stay warm, and never go hunting for aliens when the thermometer dips below freezing." He continued reading, seemingly oblivious to her.

"Flint tells me that you were out all night keeping the peace."

"Flint is wrong." He tossed the magazine onto the floor and lay back on the cot.

Kate wasn't sure what to make of this. "Do I detect a note of apathy? Or is there nothing to do in this emergency?"

"Oh, there's a lot I should do." He crinkled his eyes as he thought it all over. "Let's see, now. I'll bet the snow plow hasn't been out all day."

"That's correct."

Matt grunted. "I thought so. It's got a broken muffler. Every winter storm it roars by here at six in the morning, waking me up. This time I slept until nine. Dan and Jack must be stuck somewhere in that pickup truck. I heard they were drunk as hell last night."

Kate was growing concerned. "Don't you think you should go out and find them?"

Matt shook his head coolly. "Yes, I suppose that's what I should do."

"But you're not going to, are you?" Kate felt her anger rising unaccountably. Something was wrong here, and he wasn't telling her what it was. Everyone was full of secrets this morning and she was getting tired of it.

"No, I'm not." And with that he picked up another magazine and flipped it open.

"I've never seen you so irresponsible!" she exclaimed, marching over to the cell and staring at him with her hands on her hips. People need your help. This island is falling apart, everyone's gone mad, and all you can do is sit and read!"

He grumbled something under his breath and then added, "Yup, that's all I can do."

Kate thought it all over and finally came up with an answer. "Oh, I get it. Your feelings have been hurt and now you refuse to move. That's it, isn't it?"

He turned a page in the magazine. "Don't be ridiculous."

"Am I?" She walked over and reached through the bars, effectively toppling the magazine from his hands. "Now you listen to me, Matt Caine. Just because you experienced one of life's passages is no reason to take it out on the safety of this town."

"Passages?" He gave her a puzzled look. "What passages? What the hell are you talking about?"

"You know perfectly well what I mean—the passage into grandfatherhood."

He laughed. "You think I'm lying around here because of *that*?"

He looked so sure of himself that she began to flounder. While she thought about it, Matt laced his hands behind his head and watched her. He looked so casual and almost amused by her attitude that she looked away from him. But it was too late. She had already noticed the long, lean lines of his body as he stretched out, and was remembering all too vividly what it had been like to lie in his arms. Who was she kidding? There wasn't anything wrong with Matt. But obviously something was wrong with her.

Then a glimmer of inspiration hit her. Maybe that's

what was causing his sudden ennui. "My goodness," she clucked, shaking her head, "what a fuss you're making over me."

"Over you?"

"Yes, admit it. You feel rejected and now you're acting like a baby who can't have his bottle."

Matt sat up and looked at her in genuine amazement. "You've got one hell of an imagination, Kate. Or one hell of an ego. Do you really think I stayed in here all day because of you?"

Her heart sank. Now she was making a real fool of herself. He didn't care anywhere near as much as she thought—and hoped, she realized—but she decided to brazen it out. "The trouble with you, Matthew Caine, is that you are extremely, uh, provincial."

He blinked. "Provincial? That's a new one. What happened to the passages theory?"

She launched into a full-scale attack, making it up as she went along. "Small-town blues, that's what you suffer from. You're not in love with me, you're in love with what I represent."

Matt rubbed his eyes and looked at her. "How interesting. What, may I ask, is that?"

Kate was off on a tangent with no way of stopping. Matt just sat there listening to her as if she were spouting some lunatic-fringe religious theory that was too bizarre to take seriously.

"You have wanderlust," she concluded uneasily.

He smiled, and the depth of charm in that single smile unnerved her immensely. "I have wanderlust, huh?" He scratched his chin. "Well, I don't know about that. Wander, no—lust, yes. Fortunately, it's not fatal."

"You're not funny, Matt."

But he thought so. He began to laugh at her.

Her embarrassment dimmed as her anger grew. "You don't know what you're talking about. All you've ever done is stay right here on this nice little island, letting life go by. You must have a tremendous need to go out and challenge the world."

"No," he said calmly, "I don't. I have plenty of challenge right here." He looked her up and down. "You're not really talking about me, are you, Kate? You're really talking about yourself."

"What if I am?" she said, her eyes flashing defiantly.

"That's why you insist on leaving? You're on your way to challenge the world?"

"Yes!"

"Fulfill your destiny?"

"If you want to put it that way, yes! What's wrong with that? All you can do is lounge around here doing . . . nothing."

"You're half right about that," he agreed, lying back down and putting his hands behind his head. "Right now all I can do is lie on this cot. But believe me, Kate Brody, self-pity isn't my style." He laughed at some private thought.

"Well, you can laugh all you want to," Kate said. "But you don't see me moping around."

He gave her a thorough once-over that was most unsettling. "No, I can't say as I do. Moping is not your style. Running away is more in your form. Or should I say selling out?"

She took a step backward. "At least I'm doing *something*!" She pointed furiously at the empty wine bottle. "You, on the other hand, are back to drinking, I see."

"The wine was in easy reach of the bed," he explained. "I couldn't go anywhere, so . . ." He shrugged and an easy grin came over his face.

"So you drank yourself into a stupor."

"Hey, it seemed like a good idea at the time."

Kate was fuming. "Look at you. You're not shaven, you obviously slept in your clothes, and this place is a mess." She picked up a paper plate that was sitting on the floor just outside the cell. It contained the dubious remains of some previous meal. She tossed it with distaste into the trash can in the office. "You couldn't walk ten lousy feet to deposit this into the garbage?"

He lay back and surveyed her coolly. "No, I could not."

By now Kate was beside herself. "If someone gets hurt in this town, it's going to be your fault."

"No, it's not. It's going to be those high school kids and their fearless principal."

"Go on, blame it on a bunch of defenseless kids."

"Defenseless?" Matt protested. "You call them defenseless? They were in here last night making sure I wouldn't interfere with their witch-hunt."

"What did they do, call you Granpa?"

"Not exactly," he said. "But they did call me everything else. Do you know that idiot principal wanted to give me a blood test to make sure I was human?"

Kate took a deep breath. "I'm very disappointed in you, Matt. Look at you. Lying there like a bum. You should get up already. There's a job to be done. You're not exactly chained to a wall."

"Yes, I am," Matt answered cheerfully. And with that he raised his right leg to reveal a prisoner's manacle on his ankle. He was, indeed, chained to the wall.

Kate's face fell at the sight.

Matt shook his head at her ruefully. "So much for your passages theory, huh?"

Suddenly Kate burst out laughing. "Talk about your

clichés," she noted. "You are really chained to the wall, aren't you?" She couldn't stop chuckling. He looked like a woebegone prisoner in a Grade B movie.

"Yeah, real funny. Now would you please go to my desk and get the key from the top drawer?" He gestured to the office. "And while you're at it, see if my gun is still there. That idiot Battering was playing with it after they locked me up. He kept twirling it like he was Wyatt Earp. When I get hold of him, there won't be room for two of us in this town."

Kate wisely said nothing as she retrieved the key, noting uneasily that the gun was missing from the holster. After unlocking Matt, she made coffee while he shaved and changed clothes. He sat stonily drinking coffee while planning his next move.

Kate felt the need to apologize, but it had been unfair of him not to tell her he was chained up. "Sorry about accusing you of all those things," she muttered.

He waved her off. "They weren't all untrue," he admitted.

Her eyes widened.

"The part about being a grandparent still bugs me, and the way you acted last night did hurt a little."

Kate was stunned. He had always been straightforward, more than anyone she had ever known. But he had never been so casually revealing about himself, not when it came to personal feelings. He spoke casually, as if he were summarizing the day's events, making it easy to respond. "I—I've been thinking about that," she began, but Matt waved her off.

"I knew you just needed a little time." He spoke with his old confidence and Kate could see that nothing had really changed. Only she had changed.

"Oh. Uh—was there anything else I said that hit home?"

"Yeah," he said, grinning at her. "The part about lust." He gave her a huge wink and she tried to take it in good humor. "But more on that later. Right now I think we'd better see what's going on out there."

Kate nodded.

"Dress warm, and round up whatever food is left over at Digger's store. After we finish making the rounds, I'm going to cook us up a great dinner over at my place."

"We?" She eyed him warily. "Aren't you being a little presumptuous?"

"No," he said, grabbing his coat. "After all, what are you doing here now?"

She had to think about that one too long, and then it was too late.

"Get moving," Matt ordered her. "I'll pick you up in front of Digger's store in fifteen minutes."

Blackwell's Island had turned into a disaster area. By nightfall the roads were dangerously icy, people were huddled inside their homes, and packs of previously sane men and women roamed the hills tracking down aliens and shooting at anything that moved. Luckily there was a full moon, which countered the lack of available electric lighting.

But the night was young. As Matt drove slowly along the road, slipping and sliding at every turn, Kate kept her eyes open for signs of trouble. It didn't take long to find some. Ten minutes out of town she saw Dan Shere, sitting dejectedly on a log by the side of the road. Jack Gardner stood nearby, frantically flagging them down. He looked very happy to see them and came running over.

Matt rolled down the window and Jack hopped up and down to stay warm as he related the latest news.

"They're armed and dangerous, Sheriff," he said panting.

"You mean the townspeople?" Kate asked.

"I mean the aliens," Jack explained as if she were dense. "They have guns."

"Ray guns?" Kate asked seriously.

Matt gave her a look that silenced her at once. He opened the back door and the two men piled in. The Jeep still had no heater and the two men were shaking with cold. Matt put the Jeep into gear and a few feet down the road they saw Dan's truck keeled over in a ditch.

"They shot out my tires, Sheriff," Dan explained.

"Who?"

Jack was flabbergasted. "The aliens. Who else?"

Matt shrugged. "Maybe somebody mistook you guys for aliens."

"No, it was those little aliens," Dan insisted. "What's the matter with you?"

Matt smiled. "Oh, now it's the little aliens. How do you know they are little?"

Jack answered somberly. "Because we saw them, plain as day. The one with the gun ran up to us and fired at us point-blank. That's how we know."

"With a ray gun?" Kate asked, her heart dropping as she stole a glance at Matt.

Dan reached into his pocket and withdrew Matt's handgun. "With this," he explained.

Kate knew what Matt was thinking. The disgusted look on his face was easy enough to read.

He was also furious. "How did these creatures get ahold of my gun?"

Jack was about to answer, but Matt put up a hand and stopped him. "I'll tell you how," he said. "That idiot Dick Battering probably took one look at the aliens and dropped the gun in a panic. The creatures picked it up and started shooting at him."

"Not at him, Sheriff," Dan explained. "At my truck. The little bugger unloaded six shots at all four of my new whitewall snow tires. We careened into that ditch and turned over. I'm lucky to be alive."

"Which is more than I can say for that high school principal when I catch him." Matt was furious.

Kate turned around and looked at Jack and Dan. "Where is everyone?"

"Probably over by the hills. Last I heard they had cornered the rest of the creatures there about an hour ago."

Matt floored the Jeep and skidded along the road as he raced for the hills. Kate held on for dear life while they climbed the steepest part of the island. Finally, after ten minutes of hills, skids, and daredevil hairpin turns, Kate saw the crowd of parked cars. Beyond that about two hundred people stood around, huddled together in the freezing cold. They had obviously cornered something, and her heart began to pound again in anticipation.

Matt maneuvered his Jeep right into the middle of the hill, placing himself between the crowd and whatever was out there.

"About time you showed up, Sheriff." It was Roy Wilmot. He came walking up, followed by most of the onlookers, as everyone realized he was there.

Stan Farquil, shotgun resting on one arm, tipped his

hat. "Good evening, Sheriff. Where have you been hiding yourself?"

But Matt paid no attention to these remarks. He was looking for someone. Kate watched his eyes scanning the crowd and she shrank back. When he spied Dick Battering surrounded by his students, he made a direct beeline for him.

Dick was holding the bullhorn and he used it to talk directly to Matt. "Now, Sheriff," the principal said, holding up his arm in self-defense. "Let's not be too hasty."

Gary Sanders came to Dick's defense, placing himself in Matt's path. "Now look here, Sheriff. We didn't mean any harm last night. It's just that you were acting unreasonable and—"

Matt grabbed Gary by the lapels and practically lifted him up and out of the way. Without a word, he headed straight for Battering who continued to plead with Matt through the bullhorn.

"Let's not be too rash here, Matt," his voice blared out over the hillside. "You and I have known each other for years. We went to school together, remember?"

But Matt was a determined bull in a china shop. When he reached the principal, Kate half expected him to punch Battering in the nose, but Matt was full of surprises. He stood there calmly, staring at his adversary without a word.

Wrestling the bullhorn from him, Matt walked behind him and stood at the crest of the hill. The man stood frozen with fear.

"Let's not be violent, Matt. I thought you might be an alien in disguise. Things were a little hysterical last night after the incident with Hal's boat."

He rambled on a while longer until finally Matt lifted

the bullhorn so that it was a few inches from the man's ear.

"You are an idiot!" he shouted at the top of his lungs. Dick jumped a foot in the air.

Kate couldn't help but laugh. "You tell him, Matt," she called up at him.

Everyone else broke into laugher, and Dick Battering cringed.

"I repeat, an idiot. Do . . . you . . . hear . . . me?"

The principal squirmed and tried to back away, but Matt followed him.

"Now I want you to take your car and all these kids, and drive slowly back into town," he said into the bull-horn so that everyone could hear.

"Uh, sure, Matt . . . anything you say." He made a move to go, but Matt stopped him with a firm hand on his shoulder.

"Not so fast. I'm not finished with you yet." His voice blared out over the moonlit hill. "You and your cronies are going to spend the day tomorrow shoveling snow at the high school, the junior high school, and the elementary school, so that they may be open after the big blizzard we're going to have tonight."

A hum of delighted approval went through the crowd.

Matt grinned at the man. "Or would you prefer to spend the next six months in jail for obstructing the peace?"

Dick Battering shook his head nervously.

Matt gave a final command. "Now get out of here, and take your kids with you before I change my mind."

The principal waved the students to follow him to his car. They all piled in the station wagon and everyone watched them drive away.

Applause followed. But Matt wasn't finished. He walked over to Stan Farquil and Roy Wilmot. "Now where are these creatures?"

All fingers pointed toward a distant clump of trees. Beyond the trees was a cliff that dropped straight down two hundred feet to the ocean. There was no way for anything there to escape. It was also obvious that no one had wanted to go in and confront the creatures. They had all been waiting out here for someone or something to make a move.

Matt turned to Roy Wilmot. "Are you sure they're in there?"

Roy and everyone else nodded with absolute certainty.

Talking into the bullhorn, Matt gave orders. "Okay, folks. We have them cornered. I do not want anyone using a gun. I repeat, no guns. Please, if you have a weapon, place it down in the snow in front of you."

No one moved at first, but Matt waited, adamant in his insistence. "Come on, people. We don't need anyone getting hurt."

One by one, people obeyed. Finally the last revolver was dropped into the snow. Matt smiled at Kate in relief and she took his arm.

"I'm going in there with you," she said.

He looked at her as if she were crazy. "Who said anything about going in there?"

Kate was stunned. "But I thought—"

"Think again, Kate. They're cornered in there, right?" She nodded. "Now go back to the Jeep and get that food out. Bring it over here right away."

"*What*?" How could he think about food at a time like this?

"They're probably very hungry," he said, gesturing

into the woods. "I'm going to try and buy their trust. Get the food, please."

Kate's eyes shone. "That's a brilliant idea." She turned and headed down to the Jeep while everyone waited anxiously to see what Matt would do. But as she stepped carefully down the snowy hillside, something caught her eye from the distance. She stopped suddenly and covered her mouth with her hands in complete surprise.

The others noticed it also.

Eight bright red and blue lights were coming in off the ocean from the east.

"Maybe they're jets from the air base?" someone remarked.

But the lights began to circle backward and forward as they came over the land.

"Jets can't go backward, can they?" Dan Shere asked.

Kate nervously made her way back to Matt's side and grabbed his arm. "What are they?" she asked him in a whisper.

Suddenly a bright light beamed from one of the aircrafts. In the mist rising from the shore, it looked like a giant cone emanating from a saucer. Three other lights followed in the same pattern and began heading toward them in a slow back-and-forth movement as they swept the island from north to south.

Kate gulped. "I think E.T. phoned home."

Roy Wilmot nodded, and spoke to the sheriff nervously. "Have you ever seen a flying machine do that, Matt?"

Jack Gardner's voice cried out, "It's them!"

"Them?" Matt repeated.

Kate suddenly realized what she was seeing.

"They're searching for their comrades!" she exclaimed. "Of course!"

Matt looked at her and groaned. "You're worse than Dick Battering."

But Kate didn't care. She grabbed the bullhorn and spoke into it with a newfound authority. "Everyone, listen up. Turn on your headlights! It's more aliens in their spaceships. They're looking for their comrades. Let's let them know where they are. If we don't, they'll just roam all over the island like their friends have done, and we'll be in an even worse fix."

All at once people were running every which way. In the mayhem, bodies slipped down hills and bumped into one another as they all ran to turn on their headlights.

In a few moments the hill was lit as brightly as the sky on the Fourth of July.

"It worked!" Kate shouted. She looked over to where the blinking red and blue lights suddenly grouped together. "Here they come!"

Kate ran back to Matt and took his arm. He was smiling at her and she smiled back at him and squeezed his arm excitedly.

"I have to admit it," he said to her. "That was a very smart thing to do."

"Thanks, partner," Kate beamed. "Isn't this incredible? I'll bet no one one will ever believe this!"

"Oh, I think they will," Matt smiled. "I think Blackwell's Island is about to become the laughingstock of the whole world."

CHAPTER
Eleven

KATE'S HEAD JERKED around as she looked at him. Then
her eyes narrowed. Obviously there was something he
wasn't telling her. But the cheers and yelling and waving of the townspeople distracted her for the moment.

"Over here!" they were calling. "Over here!"

Kate looked over to where Dan and Jack were making a giant arrow pointing into the woods. Nearby,
working frantically, Roy and Florence Wilmot and Stan
Farquil had joined together to make letters in the snow.
Kate read the partial message. WE WELCOM ALIE was all
it said.

Matt read it also. "We welcome aliens," he surmised,
and began laughing. "I hope there are no newspaper
reporters in those helicopters," he said suddenly. "One
look at that message in the snow, and no one on this
island will ever be able to show his or her face on the
mainland for a long time."

Kate continued to gaze at the lights as they came closer. "Helicopters?" She looked at Matt, who was grinning to beat the band, and her face fell. "Is that what those are?"

Matt's arm went around her shoulder consolingly. "Of course it is possible that the aliens got hold of eight helicopters from the National Guard and are about to launch a full-scale attack on us."

His laughter was not catching. Instead Kate felt utterly ridiculous as the whirl of the engines drew nearer and nearer.

"But what about the aliens in the forest?" she asked, pulling away from him. "I still know what I saw."

"Do you?" Matt asked. "Are you so sure?"

"Yes I am. They came out of that spaceship, right?"

"They sure did."

"And one came into my bedroom that same night, remember?"

Matt nodded. "I remember."

"And you saw their footprints, didn't you?"

Matt again nodded. "I saw footprints."

"So? Clearly we have been visited upon by aliens from another planet." Kate looked at him, fully convinced.

"Naturally," Matt said in mock agreement. "You're so smart, Kate. You have everything and everyone figured out. Everyone, that is, except yourself."

The helicopters were now overhead and the townspeople reacted as they realized they were looking at regular, ordinary, earth-made helicopters. Everyone stood back as they set down around the hilltop one by one, kicking up huge amounts of snow dust. Kate just stood there, staring at Matt. He was smiling up at them, still grinning as if he were the happiest man alive. He caught her staring at him and the grin grew even wider.

Before she could stop him, he swept her into his arms and kissed her. Kate was too surprised to move, but she realized dimly that she didn't want to move. The helicopters were kicking up so much snow that it was like a temporary, blinding storm. Matt crushed Kate against him and kissed her again, his mouth coaxing hers into a warm, willing response. Kate gave up and leaned against him, wrapping her arms around his neck. She smiled up at him radiantly.

"What was that for?" she asked .

By now the helicopters had landed and soldiers were disembarking quickly. Everyone ran up to them at once, trying to explain the story.

Only Matt and Kate stood apart, absorbed in each other. "What was that for?" she asked again, not really needing an answer but wanting to hear what he would say.

Matt shrugged like a kid. He stood quietly surveying the scene in front of him. Finally he spoke. "I used to be the biggest practical joker on this island," he said almost to himself. "This is the first time someone has made a monkey out of me." He started to laugh, turned, and kissed her on the nose. "I think I'm finally getting my old sense of humor back," he said with a self-satisfied grin. His face was beaming. He looked at the first heli-copter, and let out a whoop. Then he waved wildly and ran from Kate's side, shouting in glee.

"Hey, Hal! Hey, Freedy! Over here!"

The sight of Hal, looking healthy and normal, filled Kate's heart with joy. Everything was going to be all right now. And Matt—he looked as happy as a little kid on the day of the first good snowfall. The combination of the colored lights and the whirling snow gave the scene an ethereal, festive air, and Kate felt suddenly light-headed.

She wanted Matt back by her side now. She forgot all about potential aliens lurking behind the trees. All she could see was Matt, running along and kicking up snow. Then she had an inspiration.

Maybe, just maybe, she thought in excitement, I could get him to come with me. Maybe he could take a chance for once in his life and leave this island with me.

Meanwhile, Matt was busy talking to the officials who had poured out of the helicopters—a Colonel Walter Harrison, three FBI agents, and a representative from NASA.

While a whole division of National Guard troops combed the immediate hillside looking for aliens, the officials began gathering information from all the townspeople.

They all listened for over an hour as Matt confirmed everything Hal Freedy had already told them. Kate was surprised that he had left out the part about actually seeing the aliens. He chose to be deliberately vague, saying only that there may have been something inside the ship that exploded.

Whatever the case, after searching up and down, no sign of the aliens was found. There were no tracks in the snow, and it seemed as if they had never been there to begin with.

"False alarm, I guess," Matt said, rubbing his hands together for warmth.

"Yeah," the FBI man said skeptically. "False alarm."

"But they were there!" George Digger cried frantically to anyone who would listen. "We saw them!" He was backed up by several townspeople, but Colonel

Harrison was more interested in public safety. "Start unloading, Sergeant," he ordered.

The helicopters had brought food and supplies, as well as tools to deal with the power outage. While the army corps of engineers headed over to restore the electricity on the island, National Guardsmen began unloading Care packages for townspeople. The three FBI agents were eager to investigate the crash sight, as was the man from NASA, who seemed as skeptical as Matt.

Kate listened as the men formulated theories that ranged from a stray meteor to a satellite whose orbit had gone awry.

Matt shrugged at all the theories as if he couldn't care less. "I think you ought to go over and examine the metal fragments at Farquil's place," he suggested.

Freedy joined the conversation at the tail end. He was lucky to be alive. According to the coast-guard report, Hal had been racing through a thick fog at over forty miles an hour when he sideswiped a coast-guard cutter. The colonel reported that Freedy had sunk both his own speedboat and the cutter. The crew and Hal had floated for hours in a life raft until the fog lifted and they were picked up by helicopter.

But Hal had lost none of his gung-ho enthusiasm. "You guys had better bring your guns," he said as if it were a command.

One of the agents opened his overcoat to reveal a gun strapped to his chest. He grinned at Hal and then exchanged a private smile with Matt.

Matt patted Freedy on the back. "You did a good job, Hal. I'll see if I can convince the town board to help you pay for the coast-guard boat you sank."

Hal's face fell. "Don't remind me, Sheriff."

Everyone laughed.

After escorting the group back to a waiting helicopter, Matt joined Kate by his Jeep. In a few minutes all the helicopters began revving up, and soon the hillside was cleared of all personnel. Everyone watched and waved good-bye as the helicopters lifted and took off, their spotlights leaving giant beams of light spewing over the island.

Matt and Kate stayed long enough to make sure that everyone cleared the area. Soon they were standing all alone on the darkened hillside, watching the remaining cars drive away.

Matt let out a huge sigh of relief as he watched the helicopters in the distance circling around the Farquil farm. "You know something, Kate?"

She looped an arm companionably over his shoulder. "What's that, Matt?"

He smiled down at her and then returned his gaze to the distant lights in the sky. "From here, they do look a little like flying saucers"

Kate gave him a playful punch. "You're a big tease, you know that? I'll bet you knew all along that they were helicopters, didn't you?"

His mischievous grin returned.

"What makes you so smart?" she asked.

Matt shrugged. "I told you, I'm an expert. Maybe next time you'll believe me."

He opened the door to his Jeep, jumped in, and revved up the engine. "Would you like to join me for dinner or will it be necessary for me to kidnap you and hold you hostage in the jail cell?" he asked conversationally.

Kate laughed and eyed the food in the backseat with relish. "How does a two-inch-thick steak sound?"

"Steak! Where'd you find a steak in this shortage?"

She climbed in beside him and slammed the door. "George Digger was hiding them under the frozen vegetables," she said. "I suspected he was hoarding food just in case this was a full-scale invasion from outer space."

"How did you know to even look for them?"

"I'm also an expert," Kate said.

Matt laughed. "Let's get going. There's going to be a major blizzard in a few hours and I don't want to be caught out here when it hits." He drove slowly down the hill, his headlights illuminating the first falling snowflakes as they danced onto the windshield. The route down the steep, winding road was quite hazardous, but Kate felt safe with Matt driving. A new sense of calm took hold of her and for the first time in three years she felt as if she was finally ready to come to terms with her life. She leaned back and took a long, deep breath, letting it out slowly with a feeling of deep gratitude.

And then something darted in front of the car.

"What the—" Matt hit the brakes hard as he shouted in alarm. A second shadow and then another flew across the narrow road, directly in their path.

"Watch out, Matt!"

He whipped the Jeep sideways, and the force sent them careening off the road and smack into a snowbank.

Kate turned around quickly to see the apparitions disappear as they scurried back into the darkness. She grabbed his arm in fear. "They're out there, Matt."

"Yeah, I already know that. I almost hit one." He put the Jeep into reverse, but nothing happened. "Terrific," he said, adding a brief oath. "We're stuck."

Kate put her head out the window and saw that the entire side of the Jeep was buried in snow. "Try again," she said.

Matt obeyed, but this time the engine died. The

motor sputtered to a halt, and Matt tried the ignition. "It's the battery," he said. He reached for the two-way radio, and then remembered that it wouldn't work unless the motor was running. "I think we've got a big problem."

Recalling her exhausting walk back to town the night before, Kate calculated the distance. "It's too far to walk in a blizzard." She looked at Matt and began to panic. But when she looked at him, she saw a man who had faced survival situations before. Hadn't he found a lost boy in the Montana State Forest? This predicament was nothing to a man who read *Field and Stream* magazine. Matt was a survivalist. An expert. He'd figure something out. Knowing this gave her a warm feeling of security.

"Are you all right, Kate?"

"I'm fine as long as I'm with you."

"Good girl." He kissed her on the cheek. "Let's sum up the situation. We've got plenty of food. I've got a gun. All we need is a place to stay."

Kate knew the answer to that one. "The nearest place is Dick Battering's house about two miles from here." She looked at Matt in dismay. "Oh, no."

Matt shook his head. "I'd rather freeze."

Kate agreed.

After several minutes of thought, Matt's face suddenly lit up. "We'll spend the night at the Sarah Campbell House."

"Is that allowed?" Kate asked. "It's a landmark, isn't it?"

But Matt paid her no attention. "It's not even a half mile from here." He thought it over, making a list in his head. "It has a wonderful fireplace with a large hearth for cooking. There are plenty of pots, pans, plates, knives, forks . . ." He reached under the seat and turned to her triumphantly as he produced a bottle of St. Emilion. "Old Faithful," he announced and handed her the wine.

"We'll need sleeping bags, or a lot of blankets, to say the least."

Matt laughed. "We'll use the Campbells' bed."

Kate looked at him skeptically. "I don't know about that. That bed is over four hundred years old."

"The entire house is. So what?"

Kate hesitated. "I don't think it's right to stay there."

"Why not?"

"Because the Sarah Campbell House is a museum, that's why. It's just not right. Besides, no one has used that house in centuries. It just isn't right."

"Is that the only reason?" Matt asked.

Kate shook her head and answered reluctantly. "It's also haunted."

At those words, Matt burst out laughing. "Haunted? Who told you that one?"

Kate thought back and then smiled at her own foolishness. "Hal Freedy," she answered.

That did it. Matt howled with laughter and so did she. But Kate still wasn't convinced.

Matt gave her one last ultimatum. "Of course we could spend an entire fun-filled evening snowbound with Dick Battering."

Kate groaned. "Let's start walking," she said.

Sarah Campbell had chosen the hill overlooking the ocean in order to be the first to see every incoming ship. Ordinarily the view was exquisite, but with no moon out, a blinding blizzard, and the temperature below freezing, Kate was happy just to arrive in one piece.

It took Matt twenty very cold minutes to thaw out the lock and find the right key on his chain, but finally they were inside. Matt lit a lantern, and effected a state of rapture when he saw a healthy supply of firewood by the hearth.

At first Kate was overcome by the task ahead of her. She was about to cook a meal in the same fashion as Sarah Campbell had three centuries before. "Well, if Sarah could do it, why not me."

Matt quickly lit the fire, which calmed her down at once. He opened the wine with a flourish and they toasted the adventure on their first glass.

As the wine settled her nerves, she perused her surroundings. She had never really been here, although she had always been meaning to come see it. The house, although carefully restored, had been originally built in the seventeenth century—shortly after Shakespeare's time, she realized with a start. There was just the one room, with the imposing hearth and the simple but sturdy wooden table and chairs, plus a small storeroom and enough room in the rafters to hang scores of dried plants. There was a curtained bed in the corner, and the Museum Society had thankfully put modern-day sheets on it and a heavy quilt.

Matt went outside and scooped up a pile of snow. He boiled it in a large cauldron, and then used it to wash out all the pots and pans and utensils.

Kate watched this performance with growing admiration. "I guess it's my turn now," she said when he had finished. She bravely opened up a can of chicken noodle soup and held it up for Matt to see. "Campbell's soup in Campbell's house," she announced, pouring the contents into a small pot and then measuring some snow in the can. "This is pretty easy so far," she added, stirring the mixture.

Matt laughed. "I don't think Sarah had a can opener. On the other hand, I don't think Sarah would have braved the ocean in the dead of winter to come here."

Kate looked at him. "If that was a compliment, I thank you."

He came over to her, put his hands on her shoulders and massaged them gently. "You're one hell of a lady, Kate Brody. I mean that sincerely."

She turned and found herself in his arms. In the next instant his mouth had descended on hers and he was kissing her with an intensity that thrilled and frightened her.

"Matt . . ."

"Don't stop me now, Kate. Not this time." He kissed her again and the passion in his face told her that he meant it.

Her head fell back and she moaned softly as his mouth teased her neck, her ear, her chin—and her desire rose fiercely, swiftly, without giving her time to think.

"I want you, Kate," Matt whispered into her ear. "And you know you want me, too."

"I do," she confessed, clinging to him. "I do."

The dam was breaking, and she knew there was no point in putting up barriers any longer. Matt picked her up and carried her over to the bed, which gave her an unfamiliar but decidedly feminine feeling. But the moment he placed her on the bed, she jumped off.

"It's freezing," she explained, rubbing her arms with her hands.

Matt contemplated this new problem and solved it at once. He reached over and removed a strange-looking metal device from the wall. It was a large brass cylinder that was attached to a long pole and opened in half like a clam. Matt grabbed a shovel and filled the inside of this gadget with hot embers from the fireplace. As Kate watched curiously, he closed the clam and went over to the bed.

Placing the hot end under the quilts he proceeded to iron the entire bed until it was completely warmed.

Kate's face lit up. "A bed warmer, of course. But how did you know that?" She nodded at him, and answered it herself. "You're an expert, right?"

Matt nodded. "I had a summer job here giving lectures back when I was in high school."

Kate climbed in and reveled in the delicious warmth. "It really works," she said. "I don't know why people don't still use these things."

She looked up at him standing there. He was gazing at her with such longing that something deep inside of her stirred. She felt very giving suddenly, and she wanted to make up for the indecision that she had inflicted on him. To his delighted astonishment, she sat up and slipped her sweater slowly over her head. Her jeans came next, sliding smoothly down her legs.

Now she was clad only in a scanty white lace bra and matching briefs, and she no longer felt the cold. Her eyes were smoky as she stretched out on the bed, inviting him to join her without words.

He didn't need any further encouragement. In a moment his shirt was off and his pants followed quickly. Kate's eyes devoured his body with curiosity and pleasure. He was taut and sinewy, supple and yet powerful. She watched as the muscles rippled effortlessly beneath smooth bronzed skin, and she yearned to reach out and touch him.

But Matt reached her first. He tantalized her with long, sensuous strokes that started at her shoulders and ran sinuously down her thighs. All the while he was kissing her repeatedly and whispering tender encouragement to her.

Kate was overtaken by a surge of erotic energy unlike anything she had ever known. And she wanted this man as she had never wanted anyone before. She reached out blindly and touched bare skin that was lightly dusted with hair. She raked her fingers down the powerful span of his chest and heard his soft moan of response. Her eager hands found his strong arms and then explored the long, lean legs that stretched beneath taut male hips.

She fell back when he unclasped her bra and pulled it easily from her body. Her breasts were ready for him, already pouting in response, and he savored them gently with his hands before taking each pink tip in his mouth. Kate spiraled into a world of sensation, her breathing ragged and heavy. She was scarcely aware of his movements when he stripped the final scrap of lace from her body, tossing it aside and sitting back for a moment to enjoy the sight of her naked body awaiting him.

Kate's legs parted in silent invitation, and he practically fell upon her. His hands roamed teasingly over her stomach, reaching behind to stroke her rounded backside and finally dipping between her thighs. She sighed and shuddered deliciously when he touched her intimately, and several long moments passed as he pleasured her there. Kate trembled and moaned, no longer knowing or caring about anything but Matt.

She wanted, needed to torment him as he was tormenting her, and she struggled to sit up, reaching for the elastic around his hips. Drawing the cotton briefs down his legs, she stared in awed fascination at the swollen manhood before her.

"Touch me," he pleaded, and she obliged him with light, feathery strokes that seemed to drive him mad. Kate felt a surge of feminine power as the unflappable Matt Caine writhed beneath her touch, but she knew it was a tenuous power. Soon she would be at his mercy again, and her desire increased with her anticipation.

Suddenly, unable to bear more, Matt flipped over and covered her body with his. He looked deeply into her eyes for a moment, confirming the bond between them. Then he stopped to taste her breasts one more time before joining their bodies irrevocably.

Kate reached up and put her hands around his neck, breathlessly awaiting his entry. But nothing could have prepared her for the swift, liquid union that took place in one smooth motion. She opened her eyes in an ecstasy of shock. Then her legs wrapped themselves around his hips of their own accord, and they began a timeless sensual dance.

Kate clung to him, her hair spilling wildly around her as she tossed her head back and forth. She felt she could not get close enough to him, finally begging him to hold her as tightly as he could. His strong arms slipped beneath her and he held her with one arm under her shoulders and the other under her hips.

They entered a new universe, one in which they were bound together on a single silken thread. Then they shot powerfully forward, peaking in a shattering explosion.

CHAPTER
Twelve

A THOUSAND SMALL eternities passed before Kate could open her eyes and make contact with the real world.

"I knew it would be like that," Matt was whispering into her disheveled hair.

"No," she whispered back, stunned by the power of what had taken place between them. "How could you possibly know. . ."

"I told you," he said with the glimmer of a smile.

Kate finished the rest of the sentence with him. "You're an expert," she said with a little laugh.

They lay snuggled together for several more minutes, exchanging little smiles and half-finished sentences. Eventually they realized they were hungry, and they got up and pulled on their clothes.

Kate tackled the seventeenth-century kitchen easily now. Everything seemed much easier. She was wonderfully relaxed, and the steaks seemed to cook themselves as she tended them over the fire.

She sat facing Matt across the antique table, exchanging long, dreamy glances as they consumed the simple but memorable meal. Finally Matt downed the last of the wine and broke the silent spell.

"Everything has changed, Kate," he said, taking her hand. "I'd hate to see this wonderful beginning spoiled by your leaving."

Kate also drank the last of her wine. She needed courage for what she had to say. She looked at him bravely, and smiled. Her smile was intended to reassure him, but Matt's eyes flickered keenly as he watched her, and he beat her to the punch.

"My answer is no," he said before Kate could utter a word.

She blinked at him. "No? What do you mean, no? No, what? I haven't even asked you anything yet."

Matt took her glass out of her hand, placed it firmly on the table and bent over to kiss her cheek. "You were going to ask me to leave the island with you." He shook his head. "I'm not going anywhere and neither are you."

"How did you—well, that's the most . . . I'm not?"

He shook his head adamantly. "This is our home."

"It's your home," Kate retorted.

Matt ignored her vehemence. He looked at her with maddening calm, summoning the authority she knew so well. "Admit it, Kate. You've been lonely and depressed for three years now."

"Longer," Kate blurted out.

Matt took her hand. "And so have I."

"Just think," Kate mused, "if only I knew that while I was lonely and depressed, you were being lonely and depressed only a few hundred feet from my tavern in the

sheriff's office We could have been lonely and depressed together."

"No." He shook his head. "It doesn't work that way,
and you know it. Lonely and depressed doesn't multiply
well. Tell me, do you feel lonely now?"

Something shook inside her. It was as if something
was dangling at the edge of a shelf and finally, with one
more little tap, fell over and broke, the pieces shattering
into dust. She looked at this man whom she had come to
trust and found her voice erupting with the force of a
dam overflowing with emotion.

"I lost the baby," she confessed suddenly.

Matt's face was startled and then sympathetic, but he
said nothing, allowing her to continue.

"After all I went through, the pregnancy ended without any warning. If I had just kept my mouth shut, I'd
still be teaching and no one would have been the wiser."

She let that hang there for a while, as Matt held her
hand and watched her.

"And we'd have never met," he said quietly after a
long silence. "If that's what was keeping you in a shell,
I think the shell has been broken." He pressed her hand
urgently. "You don't need to run anymore, Kate. It
wouldn't do you any good anyway. I'd come and find
you and bring you right back." She looked up and he
smiled. "Why don't you stay on a while longer until you
sort things out?" The smile broadened, and she saw the
old unflappable confidence in his eyes.

She gave him a long, hard look. "And after they're
all sorted?"

"Kate, I feel as if we've been together for years. I
mean, it feels that long. All those foolish tiffs we had
over the years . . ." He hesitated. "I guess what I'm
really trying to say is—"

But he never got a chance to say it. In the next instant there was the most blood-curdling shriek she had ever heard. It shocked her to the bones and even Matt jumped right out of his chair.

Kate's face was white. "What was *that*?"

Before he could answer, a loud bang almost sent the front door crashing in. They whipped around and Kate's arms went around Matt, holding on for dear life.

She watched in horror as the century-old hinges nearly buckled under the blow. And then there was another and another. Someone or something was trying to get in.

Reaching for his gun, Matt shook Kate loose and went over to the door. "It's your cooking," he said. "They smelled it and they're hungry."

Another shrieking wail emanated from outside. The wind blew in through the cracks, and the door was slowly being forced open.

"They must be freezing out there," Kate said, her voice shaking.

Matt's hand went to the lock. He turned and looked at Kate as the banging and screaming grew in intensity. "I can't let them die out there," he said.

Kate watched in dread as Matt flipped the bolt and reached for the door handle.

Her heart felt like it had stopped, time had stopped with it.

Matt gave her one last look. "Ready?"

"Go on, Matt," she said, and took a deep breath. "Open it."

Nothing could have prepared Kate for what happened next. As soon as Matt got the door open, something bolted in and made a beeline for Kate. Before she knew it, the creature had jumped on her and knocked her to the ground.

"It's trying to kill me," she screamed. "Matt, help me!"

She fought in a frenzy of panic, but the creature had latched onto her arms. From the corner of her clouded eyes she saw three others. They were attacking Matt.

"Use your gun," Kate yelled. "Shoot to kill."

But instead of hearing shots ring out, she heard laughter.

"Shoot to kill?" Matt asked calmly. "Why would I want to hurt these cute little monkeys?"

Kate wasn't sure she heard Matt correctly. The creature had her in a bear hug and was squeezing the breath out of her. "It's trying to kill me!" she shouted. Out of the corner of her eyes she glimpsed Matt's condition. He was sitting on the floor being attacked by aliens—who bore a strange resemblance to monkeys.

With one last hardy heave, she broke the creature's grip and sent it flying head over heel onto the bed. Kate watched in amazement as it jumped up and down in its spacesuit, laughing and cooing. After doing a double somersault and a backflip, it jumped back off the bed and ran over to the table.

The others followed suit, and a few seconds later all four creatures were sitting in chairs, helping themselves to what was left of the dinner.

Kate now had time to regain her senses. She gazed at the aliens in their spacesuits, noting the logo on the sides of the helmets.

"CCCP," she read aloud.

Matt laughed. "It's a Russian invasion," he announced. "I can see the headlines in the newspaper. 'Four Soviet cosmonauts disguised as monkeys attack

Blackwell's Island and make monkeys out of the local inhabitants.'"

"Monkeys," Kate repeated in wonder. She looked at the four of them, who were happily gobbling up anything in sight. "Of course," she said, "it makes perfect sense." She examined their boots and noted the size. "That explains the little footprints we saw." She began to laugh.

Matt said, "And to think that these guys have been playing cupid on us these past few days. I think we owe them a debt of gratitude, don't you?"

Kate shrugged. "I think we had all better get some sleep. We have a big day ahead of us tomorrow."

Matt threw some wood on the fire, and together they climbed back into bed, noting that the creatures were still busy eating.

Suddenly one of them turned and looked over to where Matt and Kate were eyeing them.

"Oh, no," Matt said.

"What do you mean 'oh, no?'"

A second later four very tired monkeys had jumped onto the bed. Wrestling around, they began to nestle down, under and between Matt and Kate as they snuggled down for a warm night of badly needed sleep.

Kate suddenly found herself stunned by all this. She looked at the animals in bed with her. She looked at Matt, now separated from her by a furry creature in a spacesuit. She looked out the window at the snow that was still raging down. A cold breeze blew in from the cracks at the window and a little frigid air crept in, hitting her in the face.

None of this seemed real to her. She had just made love to the sheriff of Blackwell's Island, and now four monkeys were in bed with them.

Matt was laughing. It was a simple light laugh at first, but a few seconds later it had grown and it was contagious. Kate looked over at Matt. A monkey's boot was waving in his face. He pushed it aside and looked at Kate.

"This is one story you'll have plenty of fun telling your grandchildren one day," Kate said to him.

Matt stopped laughing, but he was still smiling. "True. But I'll need someone there to back me up."

"What do you mean?"

"I'll need an eyewitness," he explained. "My grandchildren are never going to believe me."

Kate did not want to pursue this line of conversation. After pushing over a monkey's helmet, she lay her head down and closed her eyes. "Good night, Matt."

He didn't answer her. Almost home free, Kate prayed that sleep would come to her quickly, but that was not to be. There were four monkeys and a large, sexy man in bed with her. The whole scenario was unbelievable, to say the least.

Her thoughts began to parade around wildly in her head. She began to remember fragments of all kinds of things from the past three year. The image of Matt giving a parking ticket to that car that had crashed into her tavern made her smile. The image of him, one foot propped on the fender, calmly placing a parking ticket on the windshield made her laugh a little. And the way he had handled the fights in her place. He always had a way with belligerent types. He could always talk someone out of a fight before it got out of hand. She recalled that motorcycle gang and how he had chained all their motorcycles together, threatening to dump them all into the ocean. And she would never forget the story of the child he had saved in Montana, and the offhand way in which he had related the story, as if it was an everyday thing to save someone's life.

All these scenes came at her in a rush. He was a brave man, and his courage was not always appreciated —at least it hadn't been by her.

He had been pursuing her openly, and she had been putting him off. *Why?*

She pictured life with Matt, imagining scenarios in the future. She saw him coming to her tavern each night after work for dinner. Would there be dinners at home? Would there be time for children? The thought of children brought tears to her eyes.

She sat up suddenly and realized that she was actually in love with him. She hadn't wanted to be in love with him, but it was too late. She had fancied herself a free spirit, ready to go out and face the world, but that was not to be. Gazing at him in the light of the fire, she shook her head and made up her mind.

"All right, Matt. You win." She hesitated and then took a flying leap. "I will marry you."

There was no response.

"Hey," she called out. "I said, I'll marry you."

Sound asleep, Matt lay as stiff as a board. He was dead to the world.

"Terrific," Kate said and fell back on the bed.

"I'm getting married, and only I know it."

She let her eyes close. She'd tell him tomorrow.

That is, if she still felt that way in the morning.

If she had counted on a peaceful morning, she was wrong. They were awakened by the sound of many people talking outside the house. Helicopter blades whirled, and it sounded as if the entire population of the island was outside their door.

Dick Battering's all-too-familiar voice cut through Kate's pleasant dream.

"You are surrounded. Drop your ray guns and come out with—"

An angry voice interrupted him. "Please, Mr. Battering. You're interfering with procedure."

Kate recognized Colonel Harrison's voice. "Okay, folks. I'd appreciate it if you'd all put your weapons away and step back now. As I've already tried to explain to you, these are not creatures from another planet."

Kate peeked through the curtain and saw a barely controlled mob outside. A division of National Guardsmen was busily trying to keep the entire population of Blackwell's Island from opening fire on the Sarah Campbell House.

There in the front lines was Dick Battering, looking like John Wayne in an old movie. He was dressed in army fatigues and held a pair of binoculars. A gun was strapped to his side. Next to him stood Hal Freedy and Stan Farquil. They had a fishing net in their hands.

Roy and Forence Wilmot were holding up a sign saying WE LOVE E.T.S.

Behind them all stood various onlookers and curiosity seekers, many of them bearing signs. The Guardsmen had their hands full as they tried to keep things in order. The FBI men were busy arguing with George Digger and Jack Gardner about something, and Kate overheard enough of it to realize that they were talking about the old Civil War cannon that was used every Fourth of July at the harbor. It was busily being wheeled up by half dozen high school kids with Dick Battering waving them forward.

Matt wasn't laughing.

As Kate continued looking over this scene, a group of Guardsmen suddenly rushed forward, dumped a bagful of bananas about ten feet from the house, and retreated quickly.

Matt was up beside her. When he saw what was happening he shook his head, climbed out of bed, and put on his clothes. Realizing that they were about to have company, Kate followed suit. The chimps were already up, happily making a mess of the place. While Kate finished dressing, one of them messed around playfully with the lipstick it had taken from her purse. Another was busily banging pots and pans together, an ear-splitting racket.

Without saying a word, Matt took a white cloth and tied it to a broom handle. Opening the front door a little, he put it outside and waved it vigorously.

"Is that you, Sheriff?" the colonel called out.

"Yeah," Matt answered. "Tell those guys to put their guns down."

Everyone obeyed at once, recognizing Matt's voice.

When Matt was sure the way was clear, he opened the door all the way and walked slowly over to the pile of bananas. He picked one up, peeled it, and calmly began eating it.

Suddenly, in a frenzied rush, the four chimps clambered out the door and leaped onto the pile of bananas. They went crazy at the bounty and knocked Matt over in their attempt to get at their favorite food.

Dick Battering was electrified. "It's the aliens!"

Colonel Harrison gave Dick a withering look and walked calmly over to Matt. Everyone closed ranks and converged around the sheriff and the wild feeding frenzy in front of them.

Kate reached him first. She took a banana, peeled it,

and handed it to a monkey. Then she put her arm around
Matt and sat down in the snow next to him.

"Monkeys," George Digger said, rubbing his head.

"Chimps," Hal Freedy added, looking stunned.
"They used to use them in the old NASA rockets." He
looked at the NASA man for confirmation.

Florence Wilmot wasn't ready to quit. "These are
Commie chimps," she said. "We've been invaded."

Matt looked at Colonel Harrison. "What's the story,
Colonel? Were these poor fellows part of a Soviet spaceship that crashed?"

Harrison shrugged. "We got confirmation this morning. The Soviets were experimenting with a Martian
lander. It was supposed to come down in Siberia,
but—" He spread his hands wide.

"Well, they certainly made monkeys out of us," Dick
Battering laughed. He looked at Matt. "No hard feelings, Sheriff?"

Matt got up and dusted the snow from his pants.
"Heck of a blizzard we had last night, right, Battering?"

The principal didn't answer.

Matt walked over to the side of the Sarah Campbell
House and returned with a snow shovel. He pointed to
where the walkway had been. "You can start by clearing
this one first. Then I want you and all the high school
kids involved to shovel all public walkways on this island." He handed Battering the shovel. "Right now,
mister. That's an order."

Dick Battering took the shovel with a sour expression
and stomped off.

But Matt wasn't finished. He took the megaphone
from the colonel's hands and looked around at his
friends and neighbors.

"While I have your attention, folks. I have an an-

nouncement to make." He looked at Kate and smiled.
"I'm going to be a grandfather."

Everyone cheered and clapped and congratulated
him.

"That's not all," he continued with a mischievous
grin. He put his arm around Kate and pulled her to his
side. "Last night Kate Brody agreed to marry me."

While everyone cheered, Kate tried to break away
from him, but he held on tight.

"Why, you rascal," she said. "You were awake after
all."

"I'm an expert survivalist. I never let myself get
caught off guard. Do you think I'd propose and then fall
asleep without hearing your answer?"

"You didn't actually propose," she protested.

"Well, you accepted," he argued back. "What's the
difference now?"

Kate gave him a little smile. "Do it now."

"What?"

"Do it. Propose. Or I won't accept."

"But you already have!"

Everyone was listening candidly and they all
laughed.

"Do it, big shot!" Jack Gardner call out.

"Yeah, come on," Hall Freedy agreed.

Matt glared at them and looked at Kate, who looked
back at him expectantly. Then, with elaborate gallantry,
he got down on one knee and addressed her.

"Will you do me the honor—that is, would you
please give consideration to . . . oh, heck." He held out
his arms. "Will you marry me?"

In that instant, one of the chimps ran into Matt's
open arms and hugged him. Matt looked at the chimp
and shook his head. "Not you, silly."

Everyone burst out laughing, and Roy Wilmot snapped a picture.

"I want a copy for my grandchildren," Kate said to Roy. She looked at Matt. "It will be the proof we need. They'd never believe this story otherwise."

Matt smiled up at her. "Does that mean you'll marry me?"

Kate knelt down and pried the monkey away from Matt. "Sorry, chimp, but this man's taken." She wrapped her arms around Matt and kissed him soundly. "I love you, Matthew Caine."

"And I love you," he answered softly, returning her kiss. "Now come on, let's get out of here."

From the <u>New York Times</u> bestselling author
of <u>Morning Glory</u>

LaVyrle Spencer

One of today's best-loved authors
of bittersweet human drama and
captivating romance.

___SPRING FANCY	0-515-10122-2/$3.95
___YEARS	0-515-08489-1/$4.95
___SEPARATE BEDS	0-515-09037-9/$4.95
___HUMMINGBIRD	0-515-09160-X/$4.95
___A HEART SPEAKS	0-515-09039-5/$4.50
___THE GAMBLE	0-515-08901-X/$4.95
___VOWS	0-515-09477-3/$4.95
___THE HELLION	0-515-09951-1/$4.50

213